In Control

In Control

Copyright © 2018 by Cederick Stewart

All rights reserved

Interior Design:

Cederick Stewart

ISBN print: 978-1-945304-83-5

Categories: Christian Fiction

Library of Congress Control Number: Pending

Categories: Fiction/Christian Living

Chapter One

In Control

Alpha

"You see here that we need to be more aggressive in our marketing approach, if we are to reach the urban population. We have to be able to speak their language. We must know what is going on there so we can pinpoint their needs. There are many pressing items that affect them every day and that is why we have Neema Smart with us today. She will be a regular participant in our urban marketing meetings because I have pinpointed her as our expert in this field. We are a dying breed gentleman. We are getting older as this world is catering to the younger so we have our ace in the hole here with us. So, I would like to introduce everyone to her. Neema come up here and share your vision for what we are doing." Mr. Derby says as he extends his hand out to Neema as she walks up to the front of the boardroom. Neema shook Mr. Derby's hand as she stops at the head of the boardroom table. Mr. Derby was Neema's number one supporter as well as her boss. At times it seemed that his only purpose was for Neema to succeed and that made her feel so special. He was a father figure that has instilled many things and ideas in her that will help her take her career to the next level. He was the type of older person that was okay with sharing their knowledge of their craft and is not worried about losing their position to someone younger. Mr. Derby was more or less a mentor to Neema. He not only spoke to her on career matters but also life matters as well. He would go into detail on how she should present herself and her ideas to the investors. Every piece of advice spoke of how you carry yourself because sometimes that tells a greater story than what comes out of your mouth. He was serious about that in the way he took care of how he looked on a regular basis. The chiseled five o'clock shadow look that Mr. Derby displayed all the time. His tanned yellow skin was only accented by his white stubble on his face. His hair was totally white and was always at the same level. It was a tad bit smaller than an afro. He was tall, thin and very athletic which was in part to his weekly games of racquetball. Neema looked up to Mr. Derby because he was someone that could relate to the drive that Neema has to succeed. Mr. Derby had also started at the bottom some twenty five years ago. He has come a long way because now he is the Vice President of Marketing, so he can understand Neema's commitment and he knows how important it is for her to succeed. In the business world, the odds of having a repeat story like Mr. Derby's doesn't happen too often. As Neema stood before the investors, she relished the feeling she had from standing up there. The thought of finally being somebody important and the respect that comes from it. It was tough to feel respected where Neema came from since she started out as a temp. Over the past six years she has done everything necessary in order to succeed.

"Thank you Mr. Derby. I would like to thank him for giving me a chance to strengthen the marketing of our products with fresh strategies. I strongly feel that with the right strategy we can bring life to our products in the urban neighborhood. Let's talk about our new plan and that starts with our new state of the art signs. These signs are no longer the big, huge, dull and easily destroyed by weather signs that seem to be reaching into the sky. You pass by them every day but pay no attention to them and those are outdated dinosaurs. No, we have signs now that are LED illuminated so you can easily see and read our signs from a distance as they jump out at you. At night they light up the area like a firework show. They are not big square behemoths but they are multi-shaped, eye popping displays that will definitely attract attention. We have been rolling out these new design signs with our new wave of personal signs that are called, **"Free Speech Signs"**. We have marketed these signs, in the upper class areas and they have taken advantage of it by advertising their companies, products and political affiliations. They used the signs as an affordable means of revenue. The simple fact is that it is cheaper and more feasible to advertise in his or her own neighborhood. It was a way to let their neighbors know that the companies they frequent and love are owned by people just like them that live in their subdivision. The average upper class family has a side business that operates out of their home so what better way to let people know of those businesses as well. I know what you are thinking, the internet and social media groups do the exact same thing. That is true but the average homeowner notices signs in or near their neighborhoods and they make eye contact with those signs every time they enter or leave a neighborhood so the idea is to always be seen on a daily basis not like the social media marketing that can be skipped or overlooked. So, they can continue to maximize the signs to better their already thriving situation, don't you agree?" Neema asks as she awaits the head nods she was expecting before continuing.

"The middle class areas are taking full advantage of the signs by using them as a means to advertise how great their areas are compared to the overpriced upper class areas. They are not only promoting their businesses but also the cost consciousness that a stable middle class area can bring a family looking for a home. Even in politics the middle class family is described as the norm when it comes to living but they are the ones that are taxed the most. The signs help them reassure families that the middle class areas can have perks as well that are affordable even while getting the short end of the tax breaks. They want the world to know that there are perks to being middle class and that you won't lose any respect because of it. The upper class and middle class areas have found a way to promote their businesses and their lifestyles in a way that is appealing. Unfortunately those types of signs are not good for the lower class urban areas. The urban areas don't have much to brag on and they can't sell their area as a place that is a great place to live. So, what you do in areas like this is give them a voice. Our signs can be a way for them to express their views." Neema says as she looks around the boardroom for approval.

"Basically you are suggesting that we let them use these signs as a way to be heard?" Mr. Derby asks to add to what Neema was saying.

"Yes sir. That is exactly what I am talking about. These areas don't necessarily feel that many people pay attention to their needs. They feel that they are overlooked in politics and are not given enough to help fix their situation. With the signs they will feel that people can no longer ignore their plight.

"Well said Neema. Guys we have numbers and statistics to back up what was just said. If you could dim the lights on the way back to your seat Neema, I will explain the charts to everyone." Mr. Derby says as he walks up to the front of the room. Neema dims the lights and she sits in one of the boardroom chairs along the wall. She was trying to get her heart to stop beating so fast. She knows that if she can sell this marketing pitch, to the board members, it will open many doors for her. She wasn't just pitching her idea to anyone but to all the investors of the company. If they all agree then it was a done deal. Mr. Derby knew that Neema was new to the lingo as well as the way to present her ideas so he agreed to give Neema credit but he was going to narrate the finer points. It was the way it should be since one slip of the tongue could turn the presentation from something good to something that could be a liability. So Neema has no problem with playing the backseat, besides she gets to sit here and see how it is truly done. It was funny that Neema was speaking so passionately about the urban areas needs as if she actually knew what they were. How she spoke about giving them a voice but quiet is kept, she didn't care about what they had to say. Neema knew deep down inside that she despised the urban areas. She hated to watch the news to see and hear about senseless crimes. She didn't like passing thru the urban areas because the sights wasn't pleasing to see. There were the dirty and outdated buildings, weeds and trash everywhere and it always looked depressing. Neema knew she was fixated on looks and how well things were kept up. The better it was presented, the more value it would be worth. She felt that way when it came to people as well because she felt that everyone should be presentable at all times and try to look their best. She felt like most of the residents in the urban areas didn't take pride in the way the area they lived in looked and that was part of the problem. They wouldn't work together to do upkeep so that the area would look like it was of some value. Neema felt the urban areas were exactly the way they needed to be. In her mind, their situation was the way it was because they don't understand how important it was to lend a hand to help themselves out and not necessarily depend on handouts and free rides. She watched her mom and dad work almost seven days a week to make sure they had everything they needed. She went to a private school in an upscale area of Houston. She was one of twenty five African American students in the school of thirty two hundred. She went out of her way to ensure that all the other students knew she was just as smart as the rest of them. She didn't play organized sports no matter how many coaches asked her. She was an average sized kid but in gym class she was a beast and she easily beat the other girls in all the sports activities. She never wanted to be the token black on any of the sports teams, so she focused only on her school work. Getting the best grades possible was her only goal. She graduated in the top thirty of her class but was offered no scholarships and she was hurt by it. She knew she did everything she could to get a scholarship but she didn't receive any money. Neema became bitter because her parents made too much money for most scholarships and that was a tough pill to swallow. She watched some of the other African American students get scholarships because of their athletic abilities. They paraded around school as if they were truly accepted by all but Neema knew the only reason they received a scholarship was because they excelled at sports. None of them were as smart as Neema nor did they even focus on their school work so she wanted to show them she could be successful too without playing sports. She knew her parents were depending on her getting a scholarship for college so once she exhausted all funding methods, she swallowed her pride and went to look for a job. She found an open position here at **Signs for your Minds**. Even though it was a lower level position, that was temp to perm, she liked the fact that there was room to grow. So the company has been on a steady upswing as it has made strides in the industry and became very profitable. The more money the company made the more opportunities to grow became available. Most of the new positions called for the employee to have a college degree. Neema didn't have one so she attended night school until she had earned one. At the same time a larger company bought the company she worked at but they kept the name and everything the same. No longer was the owner African American, now it had an all Caucasian board of investors. So many of their products never reached people other than the investor's type. Neema saw that as a window to her success. She knew her best chances of making it were to tap an uncharted market. She wanted to set the bar and be the first to do something on her own and not ride the coattails of other people. This was her first opportunity to make an impression on the investors. It they can see a profit in this idea, it would open doors for other ideas she might come up with and she has plenty more ideas that she is waiting to deliver in due time. Neema smiled at the thought of that and as she is sitting in the back of the room, her throat begins to get extremely dry. She had already gone through two sixteen ounce bottles of water today and it feels like she hasn't had water in days. She begins to sweat as she feels the urge to have a drink, not of water, but of liquor. She looks around to make sure no one could see her as she was starting to sweat. Her stomach begin to churn as it was trying to add emphasis to what her throat was already doing. She knew exactly what was going on with her because she had been going through these symptoms for years. It has been this way since that fateful night she had her first taste of hard liquor. Normally she would only drink wine but someone at a party explained to her what she had been missing. Ever since that first drink she hasn't thought of anything else. She started out just having a drink every weekend then it grew to once a day until it got to the point to where there were drinking binges. Sometimes the drinking binges were so bad that she would skip meals just to leave room in her stomach for alcohol. Now, wine wasn't strong enough for her because she only wanted hard liquor. She was at the point to where it has gotten so bad that she thinks about drinking all the time. She would have moments of concentration to where she could do other things but most of the time it was liquor on her mind. She looked around the room again to make sure no one was looking at her. She decides to grab a napkin off of the table to wipe off her face and neck. She reaches for the napkin that is directly in front of her and grabs a couple of them and she sees a glass of watered down Coca Cola. She takes a long hard look at it and notices it has the similar color to Crown Royal and she loved that color. Her drink of choice was Crown Royal and Coca Cola so looking at this watered down glass of soda gave her that same excitement as if it was the real thing. Neema could almost taste the Crown Royal and Coca Cola and she wanted a large glass of it right now. She knows that the ratio would be 2/3rds Crown Royal, 1/3rd Coca Cola and 1/3rd ice. No matter how small or large the glass that was the mixture and she knew the routine well. First the Crown Royal and she would make sure that as she is pouring it, she is getting a smell of it as it lands in the glass. She would then hold up the glass so she could make sure that it was more than half. Then the ice came next and if there was any room left it would be for the Coca Cola. Of course that would make it less than the 1/3rd Coca Cola ratio but Neema told herself that it was the same to make herself feel better. She knew there were times there were no more than a few tablespoons of Coca Cola in her drinks. Either way, she would drink it down like it was Kool-Aid on a hot summer day. Her first glass was always the one she drunk fast. She wanted it to burn her throat and warm her stomach and she loved that feeling. Every other glass would be taken in slowly. The first glass was just to appease her need and the others were added pleasure. Neema looks up at Mr. Derby and he was still at it. He was taking his time explaining the plan, point by point. Neema trusted her plan was in good hands. She looked around the room at all the investors and they were paying close attention to what Mr. Derby was explaining. Some of the investors were taking notes and others were just nodding their heads with approval. Neema was happy for what was taking place but her mind was somewhere else. She put her gaze back on the watered down Coca Cola. She looked at the two investors on either side of the glass and both of them had their glass in front of them. That meant that this glass was up for grabs. At this moment, Neema wouldn't have cared because her mindset was to grab the glass and bring it closer to her. Without a moment of hesitation, Neema grabs the glass from in between the two investors. The investor with his back to Neema never evened noticed what took place and the other investor just nodded as if to say that it was okay if she drunk it. Neema didn't care one way or another. She was going to drink it regardless so she begins to pull the glass closer to her face. She stares at it as if it was something she has never witnessed before. She turned the glass all the way around so she could see all of it. She lowered the glass until it was below her nose and then she took a deep breath.

Neema was slightly disappointed because she couldn't smell any Crown Royal but she knew in her mind that there was none so she understood. She lifted the glass back up and began to stare at it some more. Neema's mouth was watering and her mind was telling her to drink it even though it wasn't what she really wanted.

"Neema, could you click the light switch for me?" Mr. Derby says as he stares at Neema. Neema looked away from the glass and she notices that everyone was now looking at her.

"No problem." Neema says as she gets up and walks to the light switch. Once the lights were on, everyone starts to gather their things. Neema quickly walks to the table and sets the glass down.

"So everyone, think about our proposal and let's meet in here in a few days." Mr. Derby says as the investors start to leave. They nod their heads and walk out of the boardroom.

"I think it went well." Mr. Derby says as he walks up to Neema. "Was something in your drink? I saw you staring at it."

"I think so." Neema says as she gathers up her things. There was no way she was going to tell Mr. Derby that she was trying to play a mind trick on the contents in the glass to magically turn to Crown Royal.

"We will find out in a few days what they truly think once it sets into their minds. I got a good vibe from them today, I noticed great body language from them. Sometimes it can feel like poker, to where they don't want to show their hand, they want to keep you guessing on what they will do next."

"We didn't get that many questions." Neema says as she wonders what that could mean.

"I know and that is not a bad thing. Normally questions arise when things are blatantly bad or questionable. Since there was no questions then that just means we had our basic points covered. Believe me, in a few days they will have a million questions so we must prepare ourselves."

"What do you mean? Is there more that we need to do than what we have already done?" Neema asked. She knows they have spent weeks crunching numbers and brainstorming on what to present to the investors to make the greatest introduction of their idea.

"I mean we must have something tangible that the investors can see is a need for our project. If there is no need for it, then they won't bother doing it."

"What do you suggest we do Mr. Derby?" Neema asked because she truly doesn't know what else that can be done.

"I am going to go to the local credit unions and banks in the urban areas to see about donations or loans for some of the people living there. I need to know if I can get them financial support for their signs. There is no need to target the area for signs if the people can't afford them. I want you to go to the target areas and talk to some of the residents there to see what their needs are. That way we can start to decide on how the signs will look. Can you handle that?" Mr. Derby asks as he unplugs the projector.

Neema stops what she was doing and looks at Mr. Derby. She wanted so badly to tell him that she wanted no part of the urban area. Once she heard that she all of a sudden felt irritated with her new idea. She thought that they were going to do like they did in the other areas such as just advertise to companies and send out flyers in the mail. Mr. Derby wants her to literally walk the streets and get a feel of what the residents want and that doesn't sit well with her.

"What's wrong?" Mr. Derby asked because he noticed the look on Neema's face that she was trying to hide.

"Oh nothing. I was just trying to think of the area I was going to go to first." Neema says as she tries her best to lie. She didn't like this plan because it would cause her to get out of her comfort zone. Neema can really feel her thirst coming on and she needed a drink more than ever. If this plan of Mr. Derby's is to work she will need to have her best friend with her and that is Crown Royal.

"Okay, I suggest you go to the Third Ward first and start to talk to some of the residents there. I am sure they have something to say as the city built across the freeway from them and updated the area but didn't do anything on their side of the tracks."

"That's the plan?" Neema asks as she tries to stall so she can think of something else to do besides going to the Third Ward.

"Yes. Neema don't doubt me now. Just trust me and know that I feel that this is what is needed to take our plan over the top. I wouldn't steer you wrong. Besides I want you to think about this as well. We were bought out a year ago. Normally in the first year, there are no changes or layoffs. The second year is when things start hitting the fan as the larger company starts to get rid of duplicate positions. See they have their own marketing department so we must continue to do all we can to show ourselves worthy of being kept. You and I are expendable so let's do all we can to show our worth on a daily basis as we continue to make profits for the company. So that means we need to get outside these four walls and go to the urban areas to put our foot in that market. The other marketing people won't do that but we will. They don't understand the urban market but we do so let's take advantage of that." Mr. Derby says as he finishes packing up the projector. Neema just stood there. This was the first thing that Mr. Derby has ever asked her to do that she didn't want to do.

"I will call you later. Take it easy." Mr. Derby says as he walks out of the boardroom.

"Okay." Neema says as she watches him walk out. She wanted to just throw all her notepads and presentation materials across the room. She wanted to yell out, ***"You are crazy".*** She didn't tell Mr. Derby how she really felt so she had to live with the fact that she had to go and do as she was asked. Neema knew she didn't have a choice if she wanted to ensure that she keeps her job. So she walks out of the boardroom and goes to her office to put her presentation things in there. She then heads to the parking garage. She makes it to the parking attendant's stand and she dreaded getting her car from this one attendant. It was something about him she just didn't like. She hated how he always talked slang at all times to her and even with older Caucasian people who had no clue what he was saying. He always talked about how he would put twenty five inch rims on this or that car. Neema knew she couldn't avoid the attendant because she had to park her car in the parking garage.

"There goes my fine Babygurl." The attendant says as he walks from out of his office. Neema wished there was an easy way to avoid a conversation with him. She hated the way the attendant always called her "Babygurl" and even that was mispronounced.

"Please my name is Neema. I hope you are doing well today." Neema says as she tries to be courteous but in all honesty she wanted to just grab him by the front of his shirt and tell him to get it together. She wished he was open to her opinion because she would tell him to present himself better than what he does now. Be professional, respectful and don't bring negativity upon yourself. This is no time to, "Keep it real". Instead she just has to deal with who he is.

"I'm straight Babygurl. Just up here lounging." The attendant says as he sucks on a toothpick. Neema felt like cringing because she could see the man's gold teeth. The whole top grill was gold and Neema wondered if the man tasted metal with everything he ate.

"I hate to interrupt you lounging but I need my car please." Neema says as she looks away so she could roll her eyes.

"I saw your whip earlier. Babygurl it needs a shower real bad. You can't floss in a dirty BMW. You have those tight shoes on them but they need to be bigger. A size twenty five or twenty six inch rims would put it on anotha level." The attendant says as he turns to get Neema's keys out of his office. Neema notices that he had an afro pick sticking out of his hair. That was odd because every day he never picked out his hair. It always looked like he had just gotten up and didn't even bother to do anything to his hair. The purpose behind having a pick in your uncombed hair escaped Neema.

"Be right back Babygurl." That attendant says as he takes off running towards where Neema's car was parked. Neema shook her head as the attendant had to constantly stop and pull up his pants because they were so big they kept falling down.

"Just hurry back with my car." Neema says to no one in particular because no one was around. She knew that she wanted to hurry up and get to where she needed to be. Neema was fighting her urge to just scream out loud. Her body was calling for liquor but her mind was trying to tell her body to calm down, it's coming. She was irritable, cranky and had no patience at this moment. She wasn't in a good place because of the symptoms of her body wanting liquor. In her mind she was minutes from quenching it. She could feel herself starting to perspire as she waits on the attendant to bring her car. Out of nowhere she begins to hear some music. It was a loud thumping similar to a bass drum. As the noise comes from around the corner she sees that it is coming from her car. The attendant had her radio turned up real loud and he was bobbing his head to the beat. The sight of that made Neema angry. She really wanted to leave now because she wanted to cuss him flat out.

"Babygurl you have a thumping system in that joint. All you need is some twelve inch woofers to bump you out and then you are done wit it." The attendant yells as he pulls up. Neema wanted to get in his face and say the proper way to say "with" is with an "H" at the end, but she kept it to herself and waited for the attendant to get out of her car.

"I will keep that in mind. Thanks." Neema says as she hands the attendant a couple of dollars. Neema would gladly pay the attendant anything in order for him to leave her alone. So she sits down in her car and she has to move the seat back up to her normal driving position because the attendant always moved her seat all the way back as if he was laying down in the driver's seat.

"I will holla at you later." The attendant says as he takes the dollars and pulls out a wad of money out of his pocket. Neema watched him wrap the dollars around the outside of the money wad. It was huge and even if it was just ones, thick as it was, it was still big enough to be a couple of hundred dollars. Neema didn't care because she was pulling in $75,000 a year, was single and had no children. She just smiled as she thought about her financial situation and drove off.

*   *   *

Neema drives around the liquor store until she makes it to the drive thru. This was her favorite liquor store because of the very convenient drive thru window. She drives up to the window and she blows her car horn to let the liquor store know she was there. An employee comes to the window.

"I need two pints of Crown Royal and a twenty ounce bottle of Coca Cola." Neema says as she hands over her ID. The employee looks at the ID and hands it back to Neema.

"Give me a second." The employee says as he closes the window and walks away. Neema wished he would run and get what she needed. She drove as fast as she could to get to the liquor store. The thirst was affecting her the whole drive there. It has been almost twenty four hours since her last drink. That was probably a personal record because it is not accomplished too often. Neema knew she had that meeting with the investors and she didn't want them nor Mr. Derby to know that she had been drinking. She knew better of drinking before the meeting because she drinks a lot and there truly is no way of masking the smell of Crown Royal on her breath or to keep the smell from seeping out her pores if she was sweating. So, she thought better of it and avoided drinking altogether so she took some sleeping pills because she knew she wouldn't be able to sleep when her body wanted a drink. The last time she tried it she couldn't sleep and that was almost unbearable as she kept on tossing and turning the whole night. She knows she doesn't know when to stop and that she didn't want any in her system because it would just hit her out of nowhere. It would make her extremely clumsy and her judgment would become questionable so she figured it would always be in her best interest to drink only at home. She never went to happy hour with co-workers or even have liquor at parties. She would end up leaving early anyway so she would wait until she got home so she could drink alone. Even with knowing all of that, it didn't matter in the least bit now because she was about to drink as soon as she receives her order.

"Come on man. How hard is it to just grab a couple of bottles of Crown Royal and a soda?" Neema asks as the employee walks up to the drive thru window. Neema handed him a fifty dollar bill and grabbed her drinks.

"Keep the change." Neema says as she drives off. She immediately circles the building until she could find an open parking spot on the side of the building. She knew she wasn't going to wait until she made it home before she opened up one of the two bottles. Her excitement was too much as she wanted to enjoy a drink right now. She finally locates an open spot and pulls into it and parks her car. She left the car running because she knew she wasn't going to be long. She grabs one of the pints of Crown Royal and twists off the top. She takes a big whiff of the aroma from the whiskey and she could no longer control herself. She puts the bottle to her lips and turns the bottle up. Her heart starts to beat extremely fast as the alcohol races past her tongue and down her throat. The burn was nothing compared to the euphoria she felt from finally having a drink. Her stomach felt as if she had thrown a match in there and it was on fire. The Crown Royal gave her a nice warm feeling as she closed her eyes and continued drinking. She finally stops and realizes that she almost finished off half the bottle. She knew her throat was on fire but the pain felt so good to her. She reaches into her bag and pulls out the bottle of Coca Cola. It was ice cold so Neema twists off the top and took a couple of swigs. She felt that was all she really needed to balance out the alcohol she had already taken in. Besides she didn't want to waste her empty stomach on soda when she still had plenty more alcohol to drink. The only regret she had was the fact she wished she had eaten something during the meeting. She was so nervous about presenting her idea in front of the investors that she was only able to eat a few bites of her sandwich and a couple of chips. Even though she didn't eat much that was still not going to stop her from finishing off this bottle she just opened. The other bottle was for later on when she was through doing what Mr. Derby told her to do. It was going to be her prize for doing such a good job. So she takes a couple of swigs and she starts back on her drive home. She felt like she needed to change clothes before she went to the Third Ward. She had on a business suit and she knows for a fact that she doesn't need to stand out from everyone else and it is all about comfort at this point. She was going to put on something a little more comfortable and laid back. She feels that way she will fit in but she is still clueless on how to start a conversation with anyone about the signs. Since it was her idea, she knows she better think of a way and quickly. It was only a matter of time before she would be facing her new marketing strategy head on and she is nervous about it. The pressure from knowing that her job might just depend on this working was causing her to feel nervous about what she needed to do. Neema thinks about all the hard work that she has put in since she started working there and she would hate for it to come to an end because of fear and failure so no matter what, she was going to go and do exactly what she needed to do. She would overlook the fact that she didn't want to be there because it was important that she ensures her idea is a success.

*   *   *

"Hey Neema." Torii says as she runs up to meet her.

"Hey Torii. How are you doing?" Neema says as she reaches over to grab her bag off the front seat.

"I have been waiting on you. I didn't think you would get home this early." Torii says as she stands back so Neema could open her car door and get out of her car. Torii was an eight year old girl that lived in Neema's apartment complex. She was as sweet as they come. She was just like a chubby cabbage patch doll but she was as cute as a button and Neema loved Torii's confidence that she had even though she has mentioned that sometimes other children make fun of her. Torii would constantly wait on Neema to get home from work. Torii lived with her dad in the same apartment complex as Neema. Her mom died a few years ago from an illness, so Neema felt like she was looking up to her as a mother figure. Neema knew how important it was to be there for Torii just as her mom was always there for her and she loved that about her own mom.

"I am only home this early because I have some very important field work to do."

"Do you have time for us to have a mani\pedi?" Torii asked.

"Sorry Torii but I don't. Maybe tomorrow. I just need to go inside my apartment and get changed." Neema says as she tries not to hurt Torii's feelings. She could see the disappointing look on her face.

"What's in the bag?" Torii asked as she tries to peak over the top of the bag Neema was carrying.

"Oh just some things for me." Neema says as he takes a quick glance in the bag as if he didn't know what was in it.

"Nothing for me?" Torii asked.

"Well, I have a Coca Cola but I took a couple of drinks out of it."

"Can I still have it?"

"I don't know, can you?" Neema asks to let Torii know she needs to ask properly.

"May I still have the Coca Cola please?"

"See, much better. Yes you may." Neema says as she reaches into the bag and pulls out the Coca Cola and hands it to Torii.

"Thank you Neema." Torii says as her face lights up. Neema felt that was probably the same expression she has when she gets her liquor. So, Torii follows behind Neema as she is walking towards her apartment. Once she makes it to the door she pulls out her keys.

"Okay well I will see you later. Tell your father I said hello." Neema says as she unlocked the door.

"Okay bye Neema and thank you for the Coca Cola." Torii says as she takes a pause from drinking the Coca Cola and walks off towards her apartment.

Neema steps into her apartment, closes the door and walks to her kitchen and sets the bag down. Neema grabs the open bottle of Crown Royal and walks out the kitchen. Neema walks inside her room and closes the door. As soon as the door was shut the bottle was half way towards Neema's face. She quickly removed the top and starts to chug the whiskey. She kept on drinking and drinking until the bottle was empty. She was beginning to feel much better. Her nervousness and her doubt about going to the urban area was subsiding. She was actually feeling rather confident about the matter. She drops the empty bottle in the wastebasket by the bed. She walks to her closet and grabs her Houston Texans t-shirt and some blue jeans. She quickly takes off her business suit and drops it on top of the pile of clothes that she was going to eventually take to the dry cleaners. She puts her clothes on and grabs a pair of her Nike Shox from under her bed. She puts them on and walks out of her bedroom.

"Time for me to make you proud Mr. Derby." Neema says as she truly feels like that is what is most important to her. After all he has done for her, the least she can do is do all she can for him. Neema walks into the kitchen and she looks at the cabinet and sees her other bottle of Crown Royal. She pulls it out of the bag and holds it up. She turned around so she could see the light, from the window, shining thru the bottle. Neema's eyes were captivated by the caramel colored liquid that swished around the inside of the bottle.

"Hey Beautiful. I have missed you." Neema says she begins to giggle. She could feel the effect of the first pint of Crown Royal she has finished.

"You are the best there is." Neema says she continues to admire the Crown Royal. She walks to the cabinet and pulls out a glass and sets it next to the Crown Royal bottle. She opens the refrigerator to make herself a sandwich and then she realizes that she hadn't been to the grocery store in weeks because she only had milk and some condiments. Neema had been eating out for days and she had nothing left. She didn't really want to drink on an empty stomach today because it was important for her to be functional when she canvasses the street she was going to visit. Since she had no food, she figured she would just coat her stomach with the milk. She grabs the milk out of the refrigerator and she pours about half a glass. She swallows it down and rinses the glass out. She then pours the Crown Royal into the glass and begins to drink it down.

"This has to be the highlight of my day." Neema says as she takes another sip of the Crown Royal. She was feeling good and was definitely buzzing off the alcohol. Neema was savoring every swallow and nothing else mattered to her at this moment. She was filling up with liquid courage and she felt like she was ready to go and set her plan into motion. Neema had enough courage now to walk up to anyone and start a casual conversation that would lead into talking about the signs. So, she finishes off the Crown Royal and she tilted the glass all the way up so she could get every drop. She puts the glass in the sink and turns to walk out of the kitchen when the room suddenly began to spin and she had to grab hold of the cabinets to brace herself from falling.

"Neema you are faded." Neema says to herself as she begins to laugh. She knew she was getting drunk so she waits until everything stopped spinning and she was no longer off balance. She took a step and felt fine. So, she begins to walk at a normal pace until she was at the front door. She grabs her purse she had sat by the door and takes her keys out of the purse. She opens the door and closes it. She turns to lock the door and she drops the keys on the ground. She bends over to pick up the keys and loses her balance. Her head hits the front door with a loud thump.

"Ouch." Neema says as she finally manages to pick up the keys.

"Come on Neema. You have put away more than two pints before and you were fine. Get it together." Neema says as she locks the door and starts to walk down the sidewalk to get to her car. Walking was definitely a chore because with every step it seemed to be harder and harder to stay walking in a straight line. She sees a bike that was laying down on the sidewalk smack dab in the middle of it. Neema had the common sense to know that she was at her full capability when it came to her balance so her mind was already telling her body that the bike was in the way. It seemed that every part of her body got the message except for her legs. Her legs stayed on the same course they were already on and that was straight towards the bike. So with every step her mind was screaming, ***"Go around"*** and her legs were screaming, ***"Go straight".*** So the closer she got to the bike the more she understood that the inevitable was about to happen. Neema managed to almost pick her foot up high enough over the bike but it got caught on the tire and she fell like a tree being cut down, right on the bike.

"Ouch, ouch, ouch, ouch." Neema yells as she falls right on top of the bike with all her weight. She knew that if she wasn't drunk that she would have been so embarrassed. She quickly picks herself up and dusts herself off. Neema looks at the bike and she felt like telling the bike off for making her fall on it.

"Look here stupid bike. Get out of my way. If I see you here again I will kick your butt. You got me?" Neema says to the bike as if the bike could comprehend what she just said. She just stared at the bike to show the bike she wasn't playing.

"Besides I can go faster than you stupid bike anyway." Neema says as she decides, for whatever reason, to run towards her car because she wants to prove to the bike how fast she was. So she begins to jog as she ignores the pain from falling on the bike. As she got closer to the car, her mind was telling her body to slow down and stop. Just like before, her body stayed on the course until she ran smack dab into her car. She would have fallen backwards if she hadn't grabbed the driver side mirror. Neema just smirked at the thought of what just happened to her. She hit her car almost at full speed and left a nice size dent in the driver side door.

"Hey car, you must be happy to see me. You almost knocked me down." Neema says as she opened her car door and plopped down in the seat and starts the car. For some strange reason she had the urge to turn the radio up real loud, so she obliged her thought and turned her volume up on the radio to the max. Neema began to bob her head as she puts the car in reverse and drives off heading towards the freeway.

*   *   *

"You better stop blowing your horn at me. If I have to pull my car over, you won't like it." Neema says to the tenth car that has blown their horn at her. Her whole experience since she has been on the expressway has been a series of horn blasts, mean glares and vehicles speeding off as they pass her. Neema knew she was trying her best to go the speed limit but the faster she went the more the car went out of her lane. So, she decides to go slower but she still had trouble staying within the lines.

"Why would they make the lines in the road so close together? My car won't fit in between these skinny lines." Neema says as if the roads have changed since the last time she drove on it and that is why she is having a hard time staying in her lane.

"Forget these stupid lines, I am about to get off this dumb freeway anyway." Neema says because she was about to exit the freeway. She signals to get over and without fully waiting on a space big enough for her car to get over, she just moves over into the next lane. Suddenly she could hear tires screeching as other drivers slammed on their brakes because of the sudden movement of Neema's car.

"These people can't drive. All they keep on doing is slamming on their brakes. Stop hitting your brakes if you want to drive, everyone knows that. Uh, these stupid people and their stupid brakes."

Once again Neema heard screeching tires and it made her nervous so she slammed on the gas pedal and sped off the freeway onto her exit. Neema didn't even look back as she just kept on driving. She knew the target neighborhood was just two streets up the service road. So she makes it to the first light and she begins to look around and she sees exactly what she imagined the area to look like. She didn't want to hang around too long but just long enough to get some ideas about what they truly want. When the light turns green, she begins to drive and looks for a housing development to visit. Her driving was erratic because she kept on hitting the curb with her passenger side tires. It seems that as soon as she realizes that she hit the curb, she would jerk the steering wheel the other way only to let it go again and hit the curb repeatedly.

"Who would put a curb almost in the middle of the street? That is why I hate this area of the city. They have curbs that keep hitting your car." Neema says as she hits the curb again. After a few seconds she just stopped fighting it and let her tires rub against the curb as she is driving. She passes two different developments and then she sees one that looks to have some promise because there is a bunch of people standing around. She felt that was the easiest way to just walk up to someone and begin a conversation. She notices children playing in the street and grownups sitting on cars and standing on sidewalks talking. So she decides to turn in to the next entranceway. She sees the entranceway was about thirty feet up the street and all she had to do was to slow down and she could coast into the housing development. She sees a woman standing at a bus stop on the other side of the entranceway. She wasn't too concerned about the woman because she was going to turn before she gets to her. So the closer the entranceway became the more Neema tried to concentrate on turning on it. As soon as it was a few feet away, Neema jerked the wheel and turned too sharply and she hits the curb harder than the previous times down the street. The car bounces up and it startles her so she turns sharply to get off the curb. In doing so, she tries to slam on the brakes but instead she slams on the gas pedal and the car launched forward. The car headed straight for the woman waiting at the bus stop. Neema tried to hit the brakes in time but it was too late. She closed her eyes as the woman screams out when she realizes the car was headed for her. Neema heard a thump on the front hood that eventually went across the top of the car all the way to the back. Neema still didn't open her eyes and maybe it was for the best because she would have been even more scared to see that her car was heading towards a brick wall. Everything went quiet the few seconds before impact and then there was chaos as she slams into the brick wall. On impact her airbags came out and knocked her out cold.

*   *   *

"Don't move ma'am. Just stay where you are. We are going to have to cut the car open in order to get you out. I am going to cover your head with this blanket so no sparks will hit you in the face. Blink if you can understand me." The fireman say as he talks through Neema's shattered driver side window. Neema was in pain and she felt it just about everywhere. The steering wheel was about six inches from her chest and with the deflated air bag it was hard for her to take in deep breaths. Neema looks around her and she notices shattered glass from the windshield. She sees the hood of the car smashed up and just past her car is the brick wall she struck. Immediately she thinks about the woman she hit. She looks closer at the hood and she sees blood on it and her heart begin to beat faster than it already was. She wonders if she killed the woman. The last image she has of the woman was her screaming out as the car barreled towards her.

"Okay ma'am. I am going to place the blanket over your head so do not move and don't worry. We will have you out soon. You will hear a very loud sound as the machine cuts through the metal, so prepare yourself." The fireman says as he puts the blanket over Neema's head. Neema couldn't say anything if she wanted to because she was in shock. She couldn't do anything physically but her mind was racing. She felt like she could think clearly but she couldn't wrap her mind around what all has just taken place. Then came the deafening sound of the fireman cutting through her car in order to get her out of it. She only thought for a second about the fact that she was going to lose her car because she was more worried about the woman she hit. Neema was terrified about that because she has been drinking and she has never put herself in this kind of situation before. She has had drinks on many occasions but she was always smart enough to not drive afterwards. Neema tries to think back to what made her drive over here drunk. She could have just came out here straight from work instead of drinking first. Then she remembers that coming out here was part of the reason why she indulged in alcohol in the first place. She needed courage to come and talk to the residents but all of that meant nothing now because she knew that she would have to face the music soon. She is going to have to pay for hitting someone while driving drunk. All of a sudden the blanket was snatched off of her head. Neema had her eyes closed the whole time the blanket was on her head and now as she opened her eyes she realized how bright the sun was today. She no longer has a top to her car as they cut it off and it was laying on the ground next to the car. She looks around and she sees residents standing along the side of the street. Everyone had their phones out as they were taking pictures and capturing video of what they were witnessing. She sees two fire ambulances and a fire truck along with six police cars blocking off the street. Everyone was waiting to see who the paramedics were going to pull out of the car after causing such a commotion backed with destruction. Neema had a sweeping feeling of embarrassment overtake her as the paramedic walks up to her.

"Ma'am are you okay? Do you feel any pain?" The paramedic asks as he takes a long look into Neema's eyes. He motions for Neema to open her mouth and he then checks her head for trauma. He begin to gently feel over her head and neck.

"Did you feel that? Did any of that bring you extreme pain?

"Yes I felt it but it didn't hurt."

"You don't feel any pain at all? The paramedic asked.

"Yes I do just not in my head or neck other than a headache.

"Have you tried to move your arms and legs yet?

"No." Neema replies as she gets scared for a second because she hasn't moved at all and now she was worried about being paralyzed. She begins to move her arms, legs and she wiggled her toes and she was instantly relieved at that moment.

"You don't feel any pain in your back, chest or sides correct?

"Just sore but no sharp or throbbing pain." Neema says as she is happy that she doesn't feel like she broke any bones or has in major injuries at all.

"Okay we are slowly going to take you out of the car. Please let us know if you feel anything once you start moving." The paramedic says as he motions for his partner to help him. They opened up the driver side door and shattered glass came falling out. One of the paramedics jumped into the passenger side and positioned himself so he could help lift Neema up.

"You feel okay, no pain or anything?"

"I am okay." Neema says as she moves her legs from under the steering wheel and places them, one at a time, onto the ground outside the car. She could feel the soreness throughout her body. The paramedics gently begin to stand Neema up and she was happy that she could stand all the way up. They pulled a stretcher up and they begin to walk Neema towards it when she became dizzy and almost fell down.

"Do you feel dizzy at all? You might have a concussion." The paramedic says as she looks at

Neema who felt fine other than being drunk which is what she figured caused her to get dizzy again and stumbled like she did.

"Ma'am can you tell me your name?" The other paramedic asked.

"Yes I can." Neema mumbles as she sits on the stretcher and is slowly lowered backwards so she can lay down on it.

"I didn't hear you ma'am. Can you tell me your name?" The paramedic asks as he bends down closer to Neema's face so he can hear her over what was all going on around them.

"My name is Neema." Neema yells out to make sure he heard her. The paramedic nods his head and took a long look at Neema. He motions for the other paramedic to come to him and they begin to talk. Neema was so worried about everything at this point. She has to contend with the fact she hit someone and she hopes that the woman is alive. Next, she is going to have to deal with her job finding out about what she did and how Mr. Derby will be totally disappointed in her actions today. She had so much to process but at least she was alive and is pretty much okay. The paramedics walk back over to her and they take her to the ambulance and place her inside of it.

They begin to look her over again and checking her vitals and things of that nature.

"We are going to take you to the hospital now as a precaution." The paramedic says as he lets Neema know what the plan is. One paramedic jumps out the ambulance and walks to the driver side and gets in but he didn't turn the ambulance on. The paramedic that was talking to Neema scooted away from her as a policeman gets into the ambulance and sits down next to Neema.

"Hi, I am Officer Reeks. I just need to ask you a few simple questions.

Neema nods her head and her heart was beating so fast she is surprised that they can't see it beating out of her chest.

"Have you at any time been drinking today?"

Neema eyes immediately begin to water because the reality of what all has taken place today has hit home for her. She was in trouble and there was no way to get out of this one. Now she knows why the paramedic called the other one over to him and they had their little huddle before bringing her to the ambulance. She could lie but her blood work would tell them that she has been drinking. Nothing was going to help her now but the truth. Neema felt like her career and her life was over because of her drinking today. Now she wished she never picked up her first drink many years ago but all of that meant nothing because now she was faced with reality. Neema began to nervously shake and she just let her tears fall as she understands the inevitable.

"Yes sir, I have been drinking." Neema says as tears roll down her face.

In Control

Chapter Two

In Control

Ring.

Neema starts to perspire because she was extremely nervous. She has been playing musical chairs all morning and pacing the floor back and forth. It was impossible for her to sit still no matter what she tried to do. All the while she was trying to get the nerves to make this phone call.

Ring.

She had no choice about making the phone call. It was the court's orders that she make it. She waited until the very last day to do it. Neema wasn't known for procrastinating but today was a good day to start.

Ring.

Neema wanted the phone to go to the person's voicemail so she wouldn't have to talk to anyone. She only wanted to leave a message and deal with speaking to someone on a later date. All of a sudden she hears someone answer the phone and her heart begins to beat extremely fast and her mouth went dry.

"Hello." A sweet, soft voice says and Neema cringes with fear. Even though the voice was soft and sounded so kind she knew whose voice it was.

"Yes, hi. This is Neema Smart. Is this Mrs. Stanton?"

"This is she."

Neema was clueless as to what to say next. She hadn't even thought about how this conversation was going to go even though she knew she had to make it.

"Hi." Neema says as her mind goes blank. She truly did not know what to say. What do you say to someone you ran over because you were drunk? Where do you begin to start that conversation?

"Who is this again?" Mrs. Stanton asks as her sweet demeanor was sounding irritated.

"Umm, I was calling you Mrs. Stanton to see when your rehab begins." Neema managed to say as she begins to pace the floor again. She felt as nervous now as she felt in court. The way the judge stared her down and the way Mrs. Stanton's family was giving her evil looks. The whole idea of possibly going to jail was terrifying for Neema. For whatever ever reason she was just as scared now.

"Oh it's you." Mrs. Stanton says as she realizes who it was on the other end of the line. There was an eerie silence of a few seconds. Neema swear it was like she held the phone silently for a few hours.

"My rehab begins tomorrow at 10:00am."

"Ok ma'am. I will be by to pick you up at 9:30am."

"Ok."

"Bye." Neema says as she waits to hear the same. Mrs. Stanton hangs up the phone without saying a word and now Neema was stressing. She knows she was glad to not have received any jail time but what she received feels just as bad. The judge decided to try something new due to the circumstances of this case. It was Neema's first offense and she had maintained a perfect driving and criminal record. So, the judge decides to make the punishment be something that would be even more personal for Neema. Her punishment was she had to take Mrs. Stanton to and from her rehab. Not only that but she had to actively participate in it. The judge said he wanted to make it something that would open Neema's eyes to the seriousness of what took place. The other alternative was jail time and Neema definitely didn't want that. She received a suspended sentence of ten years as long as she helps Mr. Stanton with her rehab and don't receive any more DUIs within the next ten years. So Neema is willing to do whatever it takes to stay out of jail. Even though she wasn't going to jail, a part of her was still just as scared of the alternative punishment she had received. She knows she has to face Mrs. Stanton on a weekly if not daily basis.

That interaction was one that was going to be awkward at best. Neema was now relieved that she had made the phone call and now she wanted something to relax her mind. She knew exactly what would do the trick, so she walks to the refrigerator and reaches on top of it for a box she had up there. She made a late night trip to her favorite liquor store yesterday. She sets the box down on the cabinet. The box reminded her of all her Christmas presents she received as a little girl. The feeling of how she treasured what was in the box even though she had not even opened it yet. Just the anticipation of what could be in it was exciting. She opens the box to reveal eight pints of Crown Royal. She looked them over as if they were gold bricks. She was so happy to see them that she wanted to jump up and down like a child excited about being at an amusement park. She knew that this was therapy for her. She used the alcohol like a crutch when times were hard and it was her only means of getting through certain situations. This seemed to be one of those situations where she needed it. Even though the judge forbade her to drink, Neema knew that she wouldn't be able to hold up her end of that bargain. She could deal with taking Mrs. Stanton to and from rehab but not drinking wasn't even an option. Neema doesn't have the strength nor desire to not drink. This alcohol was the most important thing in her life and she didn't want to live without it.

"Don't drink. Man you are crazy. I can control this. So what I slipped up once." Neema says out loud as if she needs any convincing to keep on drinking. She felt she made a big mistake because she didn't eat anything the day of the accident. If she had eaten something then the outcome would have been different. That was Neema's mindset and she totally believed it. She could have easily driven on what she had drunk on that fateful day a few months ago. She won't let it happen again because Neema has decided to be on guard for any slipups like the one that brought all this unnecessary attention to her drinking. So she knows exactly what to do. Neema grabs one of the pints out of the box and she sets it on the cabinet. She puts the box back up on top of the refrigerator. She looks at the pint of Crown Royal sitting on the cabinet. Neema is pretty sure that if the bottle could talk, it would be seductively calling her name. The voice would be so soothing and very sexy. It would be like a voice of a siren and it would say,

"NEEEEEMMMMMMAAAAAA."

Over and over it would call her name as if it needed to get her attention any more than it already does.

"NEEEEEMMMMMMAAAAAA."

Neema knew the voice would be one that she couldn't resist. Even though the bottle didn't have a voice it still managed to get Neema's attention. She very much wanted to pick the bottle up and begin to consume it all. The bottle just stood there on the cabinet in Neema's gaze. All of a sudden there is a knock on Neema's front door. She quickly looked towards the front door because she wasn't expecting anyone. A thought popped in her head that it could be a sheriff's deputy that was sent by the judge to do a check on her to make sure she wasn't drinking. Neema figured it might be true because it was 9:00am on a Sunday morning and no one has ever just popped over to her house at this time of morning. It seemed like something someone would do if they were trying to catch you at a time when you least expect it. Neema begins to get nervous because if that was true then she was minutes from being busted. She quickly grabs the bottle off the cabinet and the box from the top of the refrigerator. She runs through the living room as the visitor kept knocking on the door. She didn't run to her room because she figured that would be the first place they would check because everyone tries to hide things in their room. So she decides to hide it in the bathroom so she runs to the bathroom and puts the box in the shower and sets the bottle on top of it. She closes the shower curtain and walks out of the bathroom. She still hears the visitor knocking so she makes her way toward the front door. Neema pauses for a second and then she opens the door and prepares for who it might be. She swings the door open and she sees Torii and her father, Dennis standing there. She felt a ton of pressure fall off of her shoulders. Here stands Torii with a beautiful flower dress on and Dennis with a three piece tan suit on with a red tie. Neema looked at Dennis and she finally realizes how handsome he was. He wasn't model handsome but he was easy on the eyes. She hadn't paid much attention to him until today and she was glad that he has caught her eye. Normally she likes the tall athletic type and Dennis was opposite of that. He was her height and little overweight but he wasn't sloppy with it. He always dressed nice and was very pleasant with her. He had small twist like braids and she preferred the preppie look but for some reason she liked the look on Dennis. Neema quickly looked away from him because she felt it was weird to have feelings for him.

"Good morning Neema. We were wondering if you wanted to go to church with us this morning." Torii says as she looked at Neema with an excited look on her face. Neema knew she hadn't been to church in years, she didn't want to tell them that but truthfully she had no desire to go to church at all.

"I felt it would be good for you to go seeing what all took place a few months ago." Dennis adds.

Neema had a long talk with Dennis and Torii after the accident because she didn't want them to find out and be let down because of it. She made up a lie that she went to happy hour with some friends and she had too much to drink. Neema lied and said she didn't drink it all and it was so unlike her to drink that much and it was a one-time mistake. Dennis and Torii believed her or at least that was what Neema thought. The only thing Neema found strange was the fact that after the accident, Torii didn't come around that often so she felt she needed to take advantage of being around Torii today. Neema figured that going to church would make her feel better. So, she thinks long and hard about should she go and then she is reminded of what she was about to do. She was about to get her drink on and that was way more important than church.

"Thank you both but I have something I need to take care of. Maybe some other time.

"Aww, I want you to come." Torii says to show her disappointment.

Dennis puts an arm around Torii to console her. Neema watches what takes place and she is moved by it. Neema knows how much Torii looks up to her so she wanted to make her happy.

"Wait, I will go. I can always finish up what I was going to do later."

"You will?" Torii says as she begins to smile.

"Sure come on in. It will only take me a few minutes to get dressed. That won't make us late will it?"

"No we always leave home early so we have plenty of time." Dennis answers to reassure Neema that they were good on time.

Neema lets them in and she closes the door behind them,

"Okay, here is the remote and you are welcome to watch television while I gets dressed." Neema says as she hands the remote to Torii as Dennis sits down on the couch next to her.

"I will be right back." Neema says as she heads towards her bedroom. Once she was inside her room she lets out a sign of relief that it was only Torii and her father at the door. She goes into her closet and pulls out one of her business suits she wears to work. Once she gets dressed she rushes to the bathroom, locks the door and begins to quickly do her hair and makeup. Once she was done, she goes to the shower and grabs the pint of

Crown Royal that was sitting on the box and she puts it inside her purse. She looked at herself once more in the mirror and then she walks out to join Dennis and Torii.

"Dennis do you mind if I grab a piece of toast because I haven't eaten?" Neema asked because she definitely didn't want to drink again without eating. She has made it a habit to eat before she drinks anything.

"No go right ahead." Dennis says as he smiles at Neema.

Neema couldn't understand why she all of a sudden recognized Dennis today and not any other day. She knows it has been awhile since she dated. Neema felt like just ignoring the feelings because she understands how complicated that would make things.

"It shouldn't take me long at all. Would you two like something?" Neema asks as she place the bread in the toaster.

"No thank you Neema. My dad made pancakes this morning and I am still full." Torii says as she rubs her belly.

Neema looks at Dennis and Torii sitting on the couch and she begins to smile. Not only because it was a cute sight but because of how she felt towards him. It was so funny how out the blue things are starting to take a turn like they have. Neema puts some butter on her toast and quickly ate it because she didn't want to make them any later.

"I am almost ready guys." Neema says as she wipes her mouth with a napkin. She grabs a glass out of the cabinet and filled it up with milk. She downed it and was now ready to go.

"OK, let's do this." Neema says as she walks out of the kitchen to join Dennis and Torii in the living room.

*   *   *

As the preacher is preaching, Neema begins to sweat. Anyone looking at her would think that she is hot because of the suit she has on. That is far from the reason. She was beginning to have symptoms that are far too familiar that are telling her it's time. Her body was telling her what it needed and just like before the symptoms never gave her a heads up, it just kicks in the door and barges in. Her mouth was beginning to get very dry. She remembers the pint of Crown Royal she has in her purse and she clutches her purse for good measure. Neema looked over at Dennis whose eyes were locked on the preacher as he was preaching. On the other side of her was a man that was struggling to stay awake.

"Are you okay?" Dennis asked.

"Yeah. I am just a little warm that is all." Neema answers as she was feeling uncomfortable and she tried her best to not show it. She knew she had to think of a way that she would be able to drink her Crown Royal. She knows that she needs just a little to make her symptoms subside for the time being. Then an idea came to her.

"Dennis, I am about to go to the ladies room."

"Okay, do you remember where I showed you?" Dennis asked.

"Yes I do."

Neema stands up and begins to make her way down the row. Once in the aisle she put a little pep in her step. Her excitement over the fact that she was about to have a drink took over her. She walked thru the foyer and turned down the hallway that lead to the restrooms. She walks into the ladies room and speaks to the two ladies checking out themselves in the mirror. Neema did a quick wave and she goes all the way down to the last stall. Neema pretended like she was going to use the restroom so at least she would look the part. She hangs her purse on the hook on the inside of the door and grabs the pint of Crown Royal. She sits down on the toilet and grips the bottle tight. Neema smiled as she grabbed the top and twisted it off. She took a big whiff of the whiskey and exhaled in a state of euphoria. She brought the bottle up to her lips and she took a couple of quick swigs and held some in her mouth. Her intention was to just take a few drinks and that was all but she should have known better than that. Since when was she ever able to only take a few sips and that was it. She took a few more drinks and would have kept on if it wasn't for someone walking into the restroom. She began to get nervous because after all she was in a church for crying out loud and she wasn't showing any respect to it. All of a sudden a couple more ladies enter the restroom and now Neema knows it is time to get back to the service. She was happy that she was at least able to taste some Crown Royal so her body would go back to normal and give her some peace for a while.

"Okay get your butt out of this stall." Neema whispers as she catches a whiff of her own breath. She could distinctively smell Crown Royal on her breath and she knew that if she could, then anyone would be able to. Neema now feels like she has let the situation get out of hand because she made no provisions as to what to do if she did drink. Neema had no gum and now she feels like she might have to ask someone for gum in hopes that they wouldn't find out about her drinking. So she flushes as if she had used the restroom and gets out to go wash her hands. She notices that nobody was at the sinks so that gave her hope that she would have a few moments to think about a plan to mask her breath. Once she makes it to the sinks she realizes that it must be her lucky day because there were a bunch of trial size mouthwash on the sink. So she quickly grabs one and rinses her mouth out real good. She washes her hands and felt better because she might be good now. That was a close call so she grabs another one and sticks it in her purse for later and walked out of the restroom. She began to feel better with every step. It was more or less because she was able to sneak a few drinks and she felt like her urge to drink was going away. She walked through the foyer and she comes across a display shelf that had a bunch of small pamphlets on it. Low and behold there was one on drinking and Neema didn't even give it a second thought as she walked past it. She stepped into the sanctuary and walked down the aisle to the row that she and Dennis were sitting on. She scoots down the row until she makes it to Dennis. As soon as she sits down, Dennis puts his arm on top of the row behind her and it was a simple act but she felt good about it and once again it felt strange that she was feeling that way.

"I was worried about you for a second there." Dennis says as she smiles at Neema.

"There were quite a few ladies in there." Neema says as she waits to see if Dennis could smell Crown Royal on her breath. He just nodded and turned back to give the preacher his attention.

*   *   *

"Neema!" Torii says as she runs up and gives Neema a big hug. Neema actually like the feeling of Torii giving her attention like that.

"What about me?" Dennis asked as he had his arms wide.

"Sorry dad." Torii says as she gives him a big hug.

"That's my baby." Dennis says he gives Torii a kiss on the cheek. Neema had a thought run through her head about kissing Dennis and she had to shake it off.

"Torii is that your momma?" A little boy asks as he walks up to Torii.

"No she is not my momma, but I love her the same."

At the sound of that, Neema felt her heart melt. Torii had never even told Neema that before and just the way she said it so bluntly told Neema she meant it.

"Oh." The little boy says as he walks off.

"I am ready to go dad because I am hungry." Torii says as she pulls her dad's arm.

"Ok, let's go. We have to drop off Neema first."

"Do we have to?" Torii asked.

"Yes she has work to do remember."

Neema shook her head in agreement because she was okay with being dropped off because the faster she gets home the faster she can enjoy a drink.

"I do have work to do." Neema chimed in as she watches Torii's smile go away.

"Okay." Torii says without trying to hide her disappointment. All of a sudden a woman walks up to Dennis and taps him on the shoulder.

"Good morning Mr. Simmons." The woman says as she smiles at Dennis.

"Good morning Miss Baltimore. How are you doing this morning?" Dennis asks as he turns to face her. Neema felt her jealousy level begin to rise up and she wasn't truly understanding why. She never had these type of feelings for him before and now all of a sudden they are here.

"I am well. I was wondering what you and Torii where doing after church?"

At the sound of Miss Baltimore asking Dennis that, Neema's jealousy was at one hundred. She didn't know who this woman was or what she wanted but the simple fact that she was trying to spend time with Dennis and Torii was a no-no and Neema wasn't having it. So Neema grabs Torii and pulls her aside.

"Torii I think I will go with you guys to lunch." Neema says as she feels she was just being petty but she didn't care.

"Yes! Dad, Neema is going to lunch with us after all." Torii says to get her dad's attention and when that didn't work she grabbed his arm.

"What baby?" Dennis asked.

"I said Neema is going to go to lunch with us. She has changed her mind."

"Well, actually it is too late. I have already invited Miss Baltimore." Dennis says as he tries to console Torii. Neema knew she had wasted her opportunity to go and to top it all off, she lost her place to some other woman.

"Neema, I thought you had work to do?" Dennis asks as he gives Neema a look like she put him in a bind. Neema knew she was wrong for changing her mind and making him do that in front of Torii. Dennis and Neema both know how Torii feels about Neema and by having him tell her no makes him look like the bad guy.

"You are right. I do have plenty of work to do and it is important that I finish. I was trying to get out of it but I should know better." Neema tells Dennis.

"Torii, you can always come over later if that is okay with your dad." Neema says as she puts her hand on Torii's shoulder.

"Okay." Torii says as if she didn't want to hear that but Neema figured if she mentioned Torii coming to her house later that would make things better.

"I think that would be a great idea." Dennis adds.

"Miss Baltimore just meet us at the restaurant." Dennis says as he grabs Torii by the hand.

"Okay, bye Torii." Miss Baltimore says as she waves at Torii. Torii gave her a halfhearted wave and then she turned and walked off.

"Let's go Neema." Dennis says as he walks next to Neema. All the way to the car Neema was very quiet. She was kicking herself for not taking advantage of the opportunity she had. Now she was mad and it was all her fault.

*   *   *

Neema drops her second empty bottle of Crown Royal into the trashcan. Now the bottle count in the box was five instead of eight. Neema managed to knock off 2 ½ pints of Crown Royal in three hours. She felt like it was helping her fight the stress she was feeling. When she wakes up in the morning she must take Mrs. Stanton to rehab. Still that was secondary to what truly was on her heart and that was the feelings she feels for Dennis. She never could have imagined that she would want to be with him after all she has known him for the past few years and it never even crossed her mind. Here she sits and she can't get him off her mind. Neema has looked out the window at least ten times to see if Dennis and Torii were back from the restaurant. Every time she looked out and didn't see his car, she got more upset. She couldn't wait to talk to Dennis about how she felt.

"Dennis, I know I should have told you this a long time ago. I really care about you, even though I don't like those twists things in your hair that you have going on but oh well. Also you could tighten up the old midsection as well but who is complaining. I like you just the way you are after you change those two things I just talked about." Neema says as she pretends that Dennis was sitting right next to her and she began to laugh out loud and it was over the top.

"I realize now how much you truly mean to me and I want us to think about being together as a couple and a family. What do you think about that? What do you think about shedding some weight so you can look like a real catch?" Neema asked as she was cracking herself up being silly. She really didn't have a problem with his weight, she is just mad that he hasn't come home yet from eating lunch with Miss Baltimore.

"I knew you would feel that way also so come and give me a kiss." Neema says as she pretends to kiss Dennis.

"Of course I would love to adopt Torii. I will be the best mother I can to her and I will be willing to do whatever it takes to make her happy. What do you mean that I need to stop drinking?" Neema asked as she felt herself getting emotionally worked up over her conversation she was having with herself. Neema doesn't feel like she has a problem. She only drinks in the privacy of her apartment and has only made one mistake behind her drinking. She loves drinking in the comfort of her apartment because she can drink all she wants and won't have to hear anyone complain about how much she is drinking.

"I don't know why I am tripping. There is nothing wrong with me having a few drinks when I want them. I am old enough to be able to do that anyway." Neema says as she grabs the remote to change the channel on the television. She flips through a couple hundred channels until she stops on a black and white movie. There on the screen was a man sitting in a recliner with a glass of liquor. Neema begins to think about how suave the man looks as he sips his drink.

"That is what I am talking about. Look at him, he is just enjoying himself. He isn't bothering anyone. It's just him and his drink." Neema says out loud as she continues to watch the movie. The man in the movie was sitting there still sipping away until a lady comes in the room. She has a frown on her face and she is headed straight towards the man.

"Look at you. Why are you drinking?" The woman asked.

The man puts his drink down on the table and exhales.

"I am just trying to relax, that's all." The man replies calmly.

"Relax? There is no time to relax. The children are running around out of control. My family will be here any minute and you haven't done one thing that I asked you to do." The woman says as she begins to get frantic.

"I will get to it in a minute." The man says as he looks at his drink.

"No you won't. All you ever do is drink. Every chance you get you drink. There is way more to life than that. You use to be better than this but now you have no control over your drinking. You started as a "Social drinker", but now you are an "All the time drinker". You can't even function without drinking. You need a drink when you are

happy, sad, mad, nervous, upset or awake. You act like you can't do anything but drink. What do you have to say about that?" The woman asked as she stood over the man.

Neema thought for a second about what the woman said. Just about everything she said felt like she could have said to Neema as well. She could easily be the person in this movie drinking her life away. She knows she drinks for the same reasons as the woman is accusing the man of. Even though Neema was drunk, she had enough wits about her to feel like the woman was right. Neema never looked at her drinking in that way but now Neema wonders if she truly has a problem with drinking. Unlike this man in the movie, Neema doesn't have anyone telling her she is drinking too much. No one is here to watch over her to make sure that she is handling her business and that is starting to make her get emotional. She felt like she needed someone beside her to be there for her. Someone who cares about her health and her well-being and that one person is Dennis. Dennis would definitely fit that role because he is totally responsible and very caring. He would make sure she did everything necessary to live a clean life and that was what Neema wanted. Neema snaps out of her daze when she realizes the man in the movie was standing up and he was pointing a finger at the woman. He had a mean scowl on his face and

Neema was wondering if what the woman had said set him off.

"Look here broad. I can deal with many things in my life but I won't deal with you whining about me. I care about them children but right now I don't feel like dealing with them. Secondly, I don't even like your family so I could care less about them coming. I will stay in here and they can stay out there or in the yard with the dogs for all I care. Thirdly, you don't tell me when to do anything. I am the man of this household and if I want to drink, by golly, I am going to do just that. Now if you value your life I would get out of my presence right now." *The man yells as he points to the door. The woman just shook her head and runs out of the room, crying. The man sits down and he gulps down the rest of his drink. He was so proud of the way he just handled the situation.*

Neema bet he really felt like a man to tell the woman off like he did. A thought crossed her mind. If Dennis confronted her like the woman did the man, would she treat him the same way. Would she go off on him and tell him where to go? Would she forsake spending quality time with Torii to drink? Neema knew what that answer was because she is drinking right now instead of being with them. Neema wanted that thought to go away so she focuses back on the movie. She sees the man looking around the room and he gets up and walks to a cabinet. He starts to take out all of the contents and he throws it on the floor. The man frantically searches through all the cabinets until he finds a bottle, he takes off the top. He places the bottle to his lips and turned it all the way up trying to get whatever was in the bottle to fall into his mouth. He hurls the bottle into the fireplace and he slumps down to the floor and begins to cry. He was upset because he had no alcohol and he was angry at the way his wife was fussing at him. The way the man was crying made Neema wonder if he realizes the error in his ways. The man probably feels the stress he was putting on his wife and he was at a point to where it is time for him to do something about it. The camera slowly moves closer to the man as he continues to cry. The closer the camera gets to the man the more you could see the anguish on his face. He was being tormented and he played the part well. Once the camera is about twelve inches from his face, the man looks up at the camera. He looked as if he was going to confess his sorrows and apologize. The man opens his mouth as if he was going to yell.

"JULIA. COME QUICK JULIA." The man yells as tears flow down his face. Neema knew he was about to make things right with his wife. That was definitely what Neema felt the man should do. The

woman runs into the room and she sees the mess the man made. She gasps and covers her mouth.

"Where are you Jim?" The woman asked as she starts to look around the room.

"I am here Julia." The man says as he raises up his hand. The woman sees it and runs over to him.

"What's wrong Jim? Are you okay?" The woman asks as she looks him over to make sure he didn't hurt himself.

"There is something I need to tell you." The man says with conviction in his voice.

"Yes Jim, what is it?" The woman asks with compassion written on her face.

"Julia, my love, I don't have any more liquor."

The television goes black and then pops up a dishwashing liquid commercial. Neema was shocked at what the man said. She was sure the man was going to apologize for what he didn't do right but instead the man focused on what was causing the problem. Neema thought about her own situation, compared to the man's and she felt they were totally different. The man was at the point to where things were falling apart around him. Neema had only made one mistake and that was it. She was currently fixing that mistake so she knew her situations was better off than the man's in the movie.

"I can handle mine." Neema says as she starts to get confident about her drinking habits. Suddenly she hears a car door slam shut and then another one.

"Dennis and Torii." Neema says as she springs up and runs to the window. She peeks out the curtain like an old nosy neighbor and is disappointed when she realizes that it isn't them. She walks to the kitchen and she looks at the time on the microwave. Neema realizes that it has been four hours since they dropped her off. She remembered Dennis saying that they were going to eat and come right back.

"Why would he lie to me?" Neema asked herself out loud. She begins to get mad because she feels like Dennis had no reason to lie to her. Unless he was going to spend extra time with Miss Baltimore and the thought of that made her even angrier. How could he choose Miss Baltimore over Neema? Neema thought she would be the better choice but she figures she is wrong.

"See Neema, if he truly wanted you, he would have kicked Miss Baltimore to the curb.

Nope he dumped you instead." Neema says as she taps her head on the refrigerator door. She was getting so jealous about the situation with Dennis that it was only adding fuel to the fire. Neema grabs the box off of the refrigerator and she grabs another pint out of it. She looks the bottle over and marvels at the craftsmanship of the bottle maker. She runs her fingers along the bottle to slowly caress it.

"You wouldn't lie to me now would you?" No. You call me all the time and you always let me know you care." Neema says as she hugs the bottle tight.

"You wouldn't leave me for Miss Baltimore, huh?" Neema asks as she unscrews the top and takes a big gulp. She enjoyed every ounce of alcohol that went down her throat. She stops drinking and just stared at the bottle. She felt so much comfort from drinking and that put her at ease. The warming effect of drinking soothes her lonely heart.

"Okay, if you want Miss Baltimore then that is fine with me. I don't need you anyway. I have something that will never leave me." Neema says in reference to the Crown Royal. She takes a couple more swigs and then she starts to walk towards the living room. She plops down on the couch and laid back. Of all the things in the world, liquor brought her the most comfort. Not her parents with their overbearing ways of telling her what to do. Not her friends that she keeps at an arm's length so she can drink daily in peace. Not her job and how they are always asking her to step out of her comfort zone so she can make more money. The liquor does nothing but wants to spend time with her all the time. It never puts anyone first and it is willing to be there whenever she needs it. No demands, no questions asked, just quality time and the liquor always delivers a good time. Neema can't recall a bad time with her drinking. She has had the luxury of being able to drink without being sick. Even on days she has over indulged her body deals with it and she never had to be in the bathroom, throwing up, and begging God to help her. She has weathered many alcoholic storms with flying colors and for that she was very proud. Someone as tiny as her could hold her own when it came to drinking but she doesn't drink for contests but for the love of doing it. She realizes that she is the happiest when she drinks. All her cares seemed to disappear. She no longer had fears or stress when she was drinking. The calming effect that took over her body was something that she longed for all the time. She knows that she can't share her secret with anyone because they wouldn't understand. Neema feels like the man in the movie made a huge mistake by letting his wife know that he was drinking. He should have been in stealth mode like Neema is when it comes to drinking. What they don't know, won't hurt them is what Neema believes is best for anyone that tries to come between her and drinking. That goes for the judge as well. That judge just doesn't understand the mature way Neema drinks and yes she made a boo-boo and hurt someone but she was not like those people that get into wreck after wreck because they have no control over their drinking. She was not careless like them, one lapse in judgment doesn't put them on the same level in Neema's eyes. So, now she just wanted to take a little nap so hopefully she will dream about drinking because that would be her ultimate dream. She felt sleep coming fast as soon as she closed her eyes. Right before she lost consciousness she heard a knock on the door.

Chapter Three

"I don't know why you refuse to drive." Neema says to the car in front of her which seemed reluctant to drive the speed limit. It was an older model car and the driver was insisting on taking his time. He was driving slowly and it seemed he had no cares in the world and he didn't care if he backed the lane up for miles.

"Sunday was yesterday. You can't Sunday drive on a Monday." Neema yells out. She didn't want to be late picking up Mrs. Stanton. That was definitely the last thing she wanted to do because she wanted things to get off on the right foot. Besides one slip up and she could be doing jail time and that is what is stressing her out the most. Most people feel like she has gotten off easy until they realize that she has zero room for mistakes. No oops or I forgot excuses will work in this instance. She had to do it as instructed by the court and she signed off on it so she knows what to expect if she doesn't do her end of the bargain. This morning wasn't a particularly good one for Neema. She had a major headache from all the drinking she did yesterday. She has fought nausea the whole morning since she woke up and she has never had to do that before. Today would be the day she experiences nausea at its worse. On the most important day of her life she has to feel like crap times a thousand. She was afraid to eat anything heavy so she ate a couple of pieces of bread. Neema hoped that would calm her stomach down. Unfortunately Neema could smell the alcohol on her breath and that was the very last thing Mrs. Stanton needs to smell. Imagine going to pick up someone, you hit while driving drunk, smelling like alcohol. Neema really wanted to just lay on the couch where she slept yesterday. She didn't get a good night's rest at all so she was even more tired because of that fact. She wanted to sleep off the pain from her head and her extremely upset stomach. Then to make matters worse she was nervous about being in the car with Mrs. Stanton. Neema never took the time to get to know Mrs. Stanton before now. Even though the accident happened months ago, she never took the initiative to try to make today any easier. She waited until the very last minute to call Mrs. Stanton about her rehab. So, Neema didn't know what to expect. All she knows is that this is a woman she could have easily killed because of her negligence. How would Mrs. Stanton respond to a general conversation? How would Neema feel if the shoe was on the other foot, would she be able to be nice to Mrs. Stanton if she had done the same to her? Neema was now wondering what you would say to someone who you have caused much pain and suffering. Do you start by saying you are sorry? Do you ignore what happened and just pretend like it never took place? As a matter of fact, do you even bring it up since you were the cause of it? Those were the questions that kept running through Neema's mind. She just needed to have the mindset that no matter what kind of conversation she had, she needed to be nice no matter what. There wasn't much more to think about because she was about to take the exit that leads to Mrs. Stanton's house. As she takes the exit her heart begins to pound. She knew that it was because of what she did the last time she took this exit that has changed her life, for now. The thought of that is scary because she was very lucky to not have been seriously injured. She did major damage to Mrs. Stanton as she had a broken leg, fractured pelvis and had to get a knee replaced and she got that from doing nothing. She was just minding her own business, standing at a bus stop, and for that Neema is extremely sorry. Once Neema makes it to the light, that was a block and a half from the accident, she doesn't want to look ahead but she does anyway. As she gets closer to the spot where the accident took place, she notices that along the curb there are black smudges from her tires that kept on hitting the curb. So she drives along and then she sees the wall that she hit. The wall still wasn't repaired and someone leaned the bus stop sign on it because it was too damaged to stand up on its own. Neema began to feel real bad because she couldn't downplay how bad the accident was. She is looking at the damage her car did to the wall and she can only imagine how hard she hit Mrs. Stanton. If a brick wall could crumble because of the impact of her car hitting it, she doesn't want to think about poor Mrs. Stanton being crushed by her car. Neema had to buy a new car and so she purchased the newer model to the BMW she already had. Neema began to feel like she was going to throw up so she turns on her emergency lights and pulls over. She puts the car into park and gets out and walks to the passenger side and sits down on the curb. She wanted to throw up but she couldn't. She had the nausea feeling but it was backed by anxiety. She wanted to just sit there and rest but she couldn't because she needed to pick up Mrs. Stanton. Neema begin to take deep breaths to calm her nerves. She begins to look around to see if anyone noticed her, when she notices something she hadn't seen before. She stands up and she focuses on what caught her attention. It looked like a large sign over the exact spot where her car hit the wall. She walks over to the driver side of her car and gets in. She begins to drive without taking her eyes off the sign. The closer she got to the sign the more she wanted to see it. Finally she makes it to the entranceway and she could plainly read the sign but she had no clue as to its meaning. The sign said, **"Ephesians 5:18."**

Neema knew it was a scripture out of the Bible but she wasn't familiar with that one or the Bible as a whole either. The sign was totally black except for the white letters. Neema looked a little closer and she could make out an emblem in the bottom right corner that looked very familiar. Then she realized what it was; it was the emblem for "Signs for your Minds". How ironic that was because the goal was to get the residents to use signs for what was on their minds. Now because of what she did, they were indeed using them but this was not how she wanted things to turn out. She doesn't know if she should be happy or sad about this. She knows that Mr. Derby didn't mention this to her so maybe he was trying to shield her from it. All she knows is he has been taking care of her since the accident. He has not been babying her but he has been motivating her to not let this setback derail her career. They were able to secure the backing of the investors and get local funding from businesses and here is the first example of their plans coming into fruition. She didn't really know how to feel but she had no time to dwell on it because the entranceway that leads to Mrs. Stanton home was near. She makes the quick right once she enters the entranceway. She goes down about ten houses until she sees the house Mrs. Stanton described. She sees the white refrigerator and brown couch that she said would be on her front porch. So,

Neema drives past the house and turns around so she could pull up in front of Mrs. Stanton's house with passenger side facing the house. Neema looks the house over and it looks bad. The house looks to be at least forty or fifty years old. The front of the house was once painted white and the only way you could tell was because there was still spots where the paint hadn't peeled all the way off. There was a screen door that was extremely dirty and the porch consisted of cracked cement. The three steps that lead up to the porch was really just cinder blocks that were stacked on top of each other to give it a stair effect. The refrigerator had plenty of dents in it and the couch looked like it had seen better days. Neema turns off the car and gets out. She walks about five feet when she heard a voice.

"That is far enough, I will come out to you." A sweet voice said and Neema was happy that she didn't have to come any closer. She waited a few seconds until the screen door came flying open. It was like one of those police shows when the cops kick in someone's door. The screen door swung open and it slammed on the wall and remarkably it stayed open as if it knew what to do. The noise from the door startled Neema who was expecting a pack of dogs to come out of the house and attack her for what she did to Mrs. Stanton. Neema could see a person, walking with a walker, slowing coming into view. Neema immediately begin to feel bad and her heart dropped when she saw Mrs. Stanton struggling. She was definitely having a hard time walking and Neema didn't want to stand there and not help her so she moved forward to help. Mrs. Stanton shook her head no and Neema knew to stay back. She had on a blue cotton jogging suit and some white tennis shoes. She was about 4'8" and maybe ninety pounds so she looked tiny and frail. Her beautiful brown skin was accented by her salt and pepper hair that was pulled back into a bun. Her court documents said she was sixty eight years old so watching her struggle was even harder to deal with knowing she was elderly. Mrs. Stanton makes it to the doorway, clutching her purse and the walker. Neema prepares herself mentally to rush over to her in case Mrs. Stanton falls so she can be there in time. She slowly steps out of the doorway unto the porch and turns right so she can head towards the steps. Neema stood there watching because she didn't think there was any way that Mrs. Stanton was going to make it down the steps. She stops right in front of the steps and looks at Neema. Neema didn't know what to do because the last time she tried to help her she was rebuffed with a look. Now Mrs. Stanton obviously needed her help but Neema wanted to wait until she said something. Mrs. Stanton braced one arm on the pole that was on her right and then she did the same with her left arm on the pole on her left. She began to lean forward and at the same time she was trying to push the walker with her body. She kept on doing it until the walker fell off the porch and it bounced off the steps until it landed in the grass in front of the steps. Neema was confused now. She didn't see how Mrs. Stanton was going to get down the stairs even with the walker. Neema knew that was impossible for her. Mrs. Stanton lowered herself down until she was sitting on the top step. She scoots herself forward until she was able to reach out and grab the walker. She struggles to stand the walker up but she finally manages to. Mrs. Stanton gritted her teeth as she struggled to stand up on her own. Her arms were shaking and she was sweating and all the while Neema stood there like a statue. After a few attempts, Mrs. Stanton was able to stand up and she began to shuffle towards Neema. Neema just stayed in front of Mrs. Stanton until she makes it to Neema's car. Neema opens the passenger side door. Mrs. Stanton followed the side walk until she was in front of the passenger side door. She turns around and slowly backs up to the car. She put her left hand on the door and her right hand on the car and she lowered herself into the seat until she softly plopped down. She brought her legs inside the car and Neema grabs the walker and closes the door shut. She then collapses the walker and throws it into the trunk. Neema gets into the car and puts her seatbelt on. She looks over at Mrs. Stanton who has her seatbelt on already. Neema starts the car and turns the A\C on high.

"Are you ready?" Neema asked in a very concerned way after all she just witnessed. Mrs. Stanton didn't say a word as she continued to look towards her house. Neema began to feel a panic attack coming on because this was what she expected to happen and now her fears are coming true. She understands if Mrs. Stanton doesn't like her and doesn't want to interact with her. Neema knows you can't fault someone for feeling negative towards you after what you have done to them. After you have disrupted their way of life in the worst way possible, how should they act towards you? Neema has it in her mind to be extremely cautious with Mrs. Stanton in the car. She wanted to be on her best behavior while she was driving because she wanted to prove to Mrs. Stanton that the accident was a one-time mistake. She drives to entranceway of the housing development and she turns on the street to take her back to the expressway. Neema looked out the corner of her eye to see if Mrs. Stanton looked at the spot where the accident took place. Mrs. Stanton stared long and hard at the spot and that was what Neema was afraid of. That accident changed both of their lives and now there was no going back. The silence of the car ride so far was bothering Neema because she knew she deserved it but it was hard to deal with.

"Umm, where exactly is your rehab center?" Neema asks as she tries to break the silence, hoping Mrs. Stanton would say something to her.

"Are you drunk?" Mrs. Stanton asks as she looks out the window.

Neema heart begins to pound in her chest because she hopes that Mrs. Stanton couldn't smell the alcohol still in her system. If she could, she could make one phone call and Neema would be locked up for ten years and now she felt like throwing up and it took everything in her power to not do that. She was so scared that Mrs. Stanton knew she had been drinking that she needed to know one hundred percent if that was the case. She figured asking Mrs. Stanton was quickest way to know.

"No, why you ask?"

Mrs. Stanton continues to stare out the window not acknowledging Neema's question and now Neema was scared because she doesn't know for certain if Mrs. Stanton knows or not. Neema knows she needs to smooth things over quickly so she decides to apologize to Mrs. Stanton.

"Mrs. Stanton, I am truly sorry for what I have done to you. I want you to know that I mean that from the bottom of my heart. I would never knowingly hit you or anyone else. I made a poor judgment call to drive with anything in my system. I was taught better than that and I just wanted you to know that." Neema says as she focuses on driving. She figured that since she was apologizing that it would help make things a little better. She read her apology statement in court that was written by her lawyer but this was truly from the heart and Neema hoped that it would begin the process to make things better between them.

"The rehab center is on the corner of Scope and Kansas Street just like the judge told you in court and like I told you this morning. If you don't remember then you must be drunk." Mrs. Stanton says as she continues to have her head turned away from Neema. She didn't even acknowledge Neema's apology and it was like she never heard it. Neema knew she had to accept whatever Mrs. Stanton dishes out because she is the victim and not Neema. So, she knows she has to dig deep and tough this out. It was only an hour ago that Mrs. Stanton told her where the rehab center was and it slipped her mind because she was so nervous. She felt stupid for asking her that but she didn't know what else to say.

"Good that is only a few minutes away from your home. That is very convenient." Neema says and is greeted with silence. Of course it is convenient but who wants to go to a rehab center Neema thought as the words left her lips. Who truly cares about going to something that they wouldn't be going to if they could avoid it? Neema felt stupid for saying that. She needs to get it together or this was going to be the longest ride in history. Mrs. Stanton has been in the car for five minutes and already the drive was unbearable. Neema looks over at Mrs. Stanton and she sees that she wants no part of any eye contact with Neema. Neema just shrugged her shoulders and decides to focus on the road for the next fifteen minutes and she let the silence keep her company. Once the rehab center came into view, Neema began to feel better because now she wouldn't be alone with Mrs. Stanton. Hopefully her attitude will change towards Neema and she would be easier to deal with in front of others.

"Okay this is the place Mrs. Stanton. I am going to drop you off in the front and then I will park the car."

"No you won't. I am going with you to park the car." Mrs. Stanton says with a very dry tone.

"Mrs. Stanton, I am not going to leave you. I just don't want you to have to walk a long distance." Neema says as she is surprised that Mrs. Stanton would want to walk from the parking lot when she can be dropped off right in front.

"Why? You don't think I can do it?" Mrs. Stanton asked.

"After what I have seen this morning, I will have to say no."

"I made it to the car on my own right?" Mrs. Stanton asked as she looked right dead at Neema. This sweet looking lady has some piercing eyes when she is upset and Neema was trying to avoid them.

"Yes you did."

"Well if I can do that then I should be able to walk across a parking lot, right?"

"Yes ma'am."

"Well if you think I can do it then park the car then." Mrs. Stanton says as she looks away from Neema.

Neema just stared at Mrs. Stanton. There was no way this was going to be an easy morning and Neema should have known that. The tension between Mrs. Stanton and Neema is making her want to drink because she wanted to be able to numb the effects of what is taking place. She no longer wanted to deal with the coldness coming from Mrs. Stanton, and Neema could better mask her feelings too if she had a drink. Neema began to drive through the parking lot to find a space to park. Luckily for them she was still able to find a parking spot near the entrance. Neema parks the car and jumps out so she can get Mrs. Stanton's walker out of the trunk. She walks over and opens the passenger side door and fixed the walker so it can be used. She pushes it close to the seat when Mrs. Stanton looked up at her with a look that could kill.

"I was only trying to help." Neema says as she backs up.

"How? By putting the walker so close to the car that I can't get out? How is that helping me?" Mrs. Stanton asked without blinking.

"Sorry." Neema says as she watches Mrs. Stanton struggle to pull herself up. It was taking her what felt like forever and Neema's patience was running thin because she was hungry but nauseous, stressing and scared. Since it's the court's order Neema had to be here to endure this for the foreseeable future. Neema watches as Mrs. Stanton begins to walk to the rehab center entrance. Neema closes the car door and follows behind her. It seemed like it took them fifteen minutes to walk a distance that would normally take fifteen seconds. That was annoying Neema because all of this wasted time could have been avoided if Mrs. Stanton would have only let Neema help her. So once they finally make it to the entrance, Neema walks ahead and she pushes the handicap button so the doors would open automatically. They walk into the lobby area and Mrs. Stanton begins to look around. Neema looks at her watch and she sees they are ten minutes late so she knew she had to speed things up.

"The front desk is over there." Neema says as she points to the desk where someone was sitting.

"Do I have on dark shades? Have I not made it this far by seeing? I can see thank you very much." Mrs. Stanton snaps. Neema didn't know what to say or do so she just stood there. She has tried to be nice and cordial and that has gotten her nowhere. Neema knew that if Mrs. Stanton makes one phone call to the judge then she would be in big trouble. That means that Neema needs to keep her true feelings to herself. She watches Mrs. Stanton slowly walk towards the front desk and Neema felt like picking up Mrs. Stanton and carrying her to the desk because it was almost unbearable to watch her walk this slowly. All of a sudden a nurse gets up from behind the front desk, with a wheel chair, and pushes it towards Mrs.

Stanton. Neema was waiting on Mrs. Stanton to snap at the nurse as she has done to her.

"Ma'am let me help you." The nurse say as she walks up to Mrs. Stanton.

"Thank you nurse. I was getting weak from walking from the parking lot to the building." Mrs. Stanton says in the sweetest voice and Neema wanted to yell out but she didn't. Mrs. Stanton sits down in the wheelchair and hands the walker to Neema.

"Why? We have a clearly marked drop off area in the front circle." The nurse says as she looks back at Neema.

"I tried to tell her but she didn't listen." Mrs. Stanton says as she rolls her eyes at Neema.

"Well ma'am just call me next time and I will come out and get you. That is ridiculous." The nurse says as she shakes her head in disgust.

"Oh thank you so much nurse." Mrs. Stanton says and Neema doesn't know what to say. She is looking like the bad guy more and more and she is powerless to do anything.

"Oh you are welcome." The nurse says as she begins to push Mrs. Stanton to the front desk. She then grabs a clipboard and a pen.

"Okay ma'am. I need you to fill out this paperwork. Is this your first time here?" The nurse asks Mrs. Stanton.

"Yes it is."

"Okay then I need for you to also fill out these two forms as well and that should take care of that."

"Yes ma'am." Mrs. Stanton says as she gives the nurse her undivided attention. Neema couldn't even get eye contact but the nurse can. That was really working Neema's nerves and she can sense that Mrs. Stanton knows it. The nurse looks up at Neema and she sees how close she was standing to Mrs. Stanton.

"Oh is this your daughter?" The nurse asked Mrs. Stanton.

"No I am just a friend." Neema answers before Mrs. Stanton says anything. She was hoping that Mrs. Stanton wouldn't say anything since she answered the question.

"Okay." The nurse says as she continues to straighten the paper up for Mrs. Stanton on the clipboard.

"She is not my daughter or my friend. She is an alcoholic that drove under the influence and hit me with her car as I was standing at a bus stop. She went before a judge and this is her punishment. She has to bring me to and from rehab as well as help me with it. That was what she received instead of jail time which she deserved." Mrs. Stanton tells the nurse as she looks at Neema with a shocked look on her face. Neema bet she had the same look on her face because she was totally shocked by what Mrs. Stanton said. Not that she wasn't telling the truth but the fact that she said it really told Neema how Mrs. Stanton feels about her being here. Now Neema understands where the attitude is coming from. Neema just stared at Mrs. Stanton as she finishes up her paperwork and for once she wished she was invisible or that she could go and sit in the car.

"Here are a few more things to fill out. I have more patients that are coming in so you can sit in the waiting area until you are done."

"Okay nurse thank you so much for all your help."

"Don't mention it Mrs. Stanton. Can you at least help her to the waiting area please?" The nurse asked Neema with major attitude. Neema didn't even reply she just grabbed the wheelchair's handles and pushes Mrs. Stanton to an area near the chairs that had room for the wheelchair. She parks Mrs. Stanton and she sits down in a chair next to her. Neema counts to ten because she can feel her anger rising and she didn't like to be embarrassed and Mrs. Stanton was going out of her way to make sure she embarrasses Neema every chance she gets.

"Could you please go sit over there?" Mrs. Stanton yells as she stares at Neema with a mean look on her face. She was no longer the sweet old lady that was talking to the nurse. Neema let out a deep sign and she moves to a chair that was across from Mrs. Stanton. Everyone else in the waiting area was staring at Neema as she sat in the chair wanting to say something so badly but she had to literally bite her tongue to stop her from losing it and going off.

"Are you happy now?" Neema snapped as she sat back in her chair.

"What do you think?" Mrs. Stanton snaps back.

"I think you are trying your best to get on my nerves." Neema says as her anger is getting the best of her. Her head was pounding, stomach was upset and to top it off, Mrs. Stanton's attitude is icing on the getting on Neema's last nerve cake.

"Look, I am about to tell you one thing right now. Don't you even think for a second that I like what is taking place? Do you think I want to be here? Do you think I want to continue to learn how to do something all over again? Something that I have been doing for sixty eight years. I have been walking my whole life and now I have to learn how to do it and you complain because you feel like I am treating you bad. I have been independent my whole life and now I need you to help me and you are upset that I don't want to sit next to you. Well, let me tell you what makes me upset. What makes me upset is when someone can drive drunk, run you over and get no jail time. What makes me upset is that someone who has caused so much pain expects to receive none as if they don't deserve any. What makes me upset is that a judge thinks they are punishing someone by making them help their victim and not realizing that this isn't helping the victim at all. Do you think I want to ride in the car with you? Do you think I want to be friends with someone that puts other people's lives in jeopardy over some alcohol? Do you really think I care about making you upset? I don't care about anything you feel right now. All I know is that I have to learn how to walk again and that is all I care about." Mrs. Stanton says as she finishes filling out her paperwork. She had finally made it perfectly clear what her frustrations were and Neema could see the pain in Mrs. Stanton's face. Neema felt so stupid to complain about Mrs.

Stanton getting on her nerves because now she understands. The way Mrs. Stanton explained it was a way Neema never looked at it before. She felt ashamed for thinking what she had been thinking about Mrs. Stanton. Neema's problems don't compare to Mrs. Stanton's issues. The second Neema thought that she begins to sweat. Anytime she feels too worked up or too down she kicks start her urge to drink. She felt the urge coming on and there was no way she was going to quench it this time. She was on her own right now because there was no way she was going to drink in front of Mrs. Stanton. Neema purposely didn't bring any alcohol with her for this reason. She knew she would be tempted and she didn't want to give in to it. Giving in would mean a one way ticket to jail and that was not an option. So, Neema stands up and walks to the refreshment area they had set up for visitors. She walks over to the coffee pot and she pours herself a large cup of coffee. She didn't want any sugar or cream, just straight coffee. She ended up drinking the coffee fast because it was only warm but she needed something on her stomach. She wanted to just stand over here and avoid Mrs. Stanton because she was right about everything she said and Neema should be ashamed for complaining about anything since she is a free woman.

"Swallow your pride, Neema. You can do it." Neema says as she turns around and sees Mrs. Stanton staring at her. Neema wondered what she did wrong now because that was the look Mrs. Stanton was giving her. She was over here minding her own business, not bothering anyone but Mrs. Stanton was giving her a look like Neema stole the coffee. So she walks back over to her.

"Do you need something? You want some coffee or some water?" Neema asked.

"Yes, I need your address."

Neema writes down her address on all the spaces that she needed to. Her hand was shaking because she was just about to have a nervous breakdown dealing with Mrs. Stanton. They haven't even began the rehab session yet and Neema's stress level was up and her patience level was all the way down.

"Is that all?"

"I need your credit card information."

"For what?" Neema says as she begins to feel her anger rising to the point to where she almost said a four letter word starting with "S".

"They won't see me without an insurance card or a credit card. I need one of them in order to do my rehab." Mrs. Stanton says in a dry tone.

"Use your own insurance." Neema says as she begins to think that Mrs. Stanton is trying to take advantage of the situation. Besides, Mrs. Stanton is not on Neema's insurance so she can't just use it. Now, Neema realizes that she was at fault for what took place but she doesn't want to pay for the rehab. This facility is one of the most expensive ones in Houston and she doesn't want to be stuck with the bill.

"I don't have any insurance."

"Why not? You have a job and as a matter of fact you have been there twenty three years. So you should have something." Neema says to show Mrs. Stanton that she wasn't going to be paying her rehab bill. Neema wasn't going to be pushed around because she was backed into a corner. She felt that enough is enough.

"If you have an issue with paying for this rehab that is fine. Let's call the judge and let's see what he says about it. Since you mentioned it I will tell you that I no longer have a job. I worked at a small mom and pops store and yes it was for twenty three years. The owner could not afford insurance for us so we all had to fend for ourselves. I haven't worked in two months so therefore I can't afford my premiums. All of that is the trickle-down effect because one person decided that it was okay to drink and drive. So no I don't have any insurance and I don't have a job." Mrs. Stanton says as she looks at Neema with a sad look on her face. This accident has taken a huge toil on her and it was apparent to Neema now. Neema is beginning to see the totality of her error in judgment. She didn't realize Mrs. Stanton's situation was this bad. All of this is putting stress on Mrs. Stanton and Neema understands why she is so hostile. She has basically lost everything all at once and Neema lost nothing and she was the cause of it all. Neema knew she was being selfish because if it wasn't for her actions, Mrs. Stanton would still be at work and her life wouldn't be so hard besides it is not like Neema can't afford to pay for the rehab.

"Okay Mrs. Stanton. I will pay for it." Neema says as she fills out the paperwork and hands it back to Mrs. Stanton. Neema sat down and she couldn't wait to get back home because she was going to drink herself to sleep. Just driving over here was a chore and filling out the paperwork was painful. She figured the actually physical rehab was going to be the worst thing she has ever experienced and as the nurse calls out Mrs. Stanton's name, Neema realizes her nightmare was about to begin.

In Control

*   *   *

Neema walks in her front door and closes it. She just stands there as she soaks in one of her most emotionally toughest days of her entire life. She begins to cry because the day had been one big huge rollercoaster of emotions and she was just glad to be home. She walks to her sofa and plops down on it. She was sitting on the same spot from last night. She was just thinking about how her day started with her waking up right here with a pounding headache. Her headache felt like a migraine and it was beating like it had a heartbeat. It felt like if she had a thought it would bring her pain. Her stomach was on eject mode for anything that was in her stomach which was nothing but Crown Royal and her body definitely didn't want to get rid of that. She fought nausea all morning and she had to take a super long shower to mask the alcohol smell seeping out her pores. She sat on pins and needles all the way to Mrs. Stanton's house. There she sees her sign idea being displayed for all to see at the spot of the destruction that she caused. Then she had to put up with the ride of death before rehab. She had to listen to Mrs. Stanton's tirade before, during and after rehab. Once Mrs. Stanton made it into her house, Neema drove off as fast and safely as she could and now she was back home, exhausted. This judge's punishment is worse than Neema imagined. When the judge first laid out the sentence, Neema was ecstatic because she avoided a long stay in jail. She figured that she could handle a few moments with Mrs. Stanton because she had such a sweet demeanor in court but Neema knows she has another side to her. That other side had Neema going through a bevy of feelings all day and because of that Neema felt like she deserved to have a drink to celebrate her surviving the day. Neema sees the empty pint of Crown Royal and her mouth begins to water but she told herself no. Neema had just told herself as she was driving home that maybe she needs to cut back on drinking. After all it was because of her drinking that she was going through what she was. The way Mrs. Stanton was constantly calling her an alcoholic, it began to sink in that she might be one. She might have a serious issue with drinking and that she needs to find a way to control it and why not start today. She has made it this long without it so she didn't need it to survive. She just needs to ignore the urges like she did earlier. She was under pressure but she was able to control it and that gave her hope that she could do it now. Drinking has always been her answer to pressure and every time she did it she believed it was helping when obviously it was hurting her.

"No I won't give in. I will not break down under pressure. I can do this." Neema says as she grabs the remote control and turns on the television. She flips through the stations until she comes to one that is appealing. It was a cooking show and it was one of her favorites. She has used recipes that she has seen on the show numerous times. Neema was all caught up in the show until a commercial came on. It was a commercial for Crown Royal and Neema didn't realize it but she actually sat up at the sight of the commercial. Suddenly her thirst kicked in to high gear and she could feel her stomach rumbling. It was no longer upset like it was earlier, now it was a different but familiar feeling. Neema's mind told her to change the channel but she didn't listen. Her hand stayed on the remote but she wouldn't press the buttons. The commercial wouldn't let her leave and her eyes widened as the Crown Royal was being poured over ice in a clear glass. The camera gave her a close up view of it and it looked so delicious. Without truly realizing what was happening, Neema stood up and walked into the kitchen. She was going straight to the box that had her pints in it. Neema felt like a robot that was being controlled by someone else. She grabs the box off of the refrigerator and opens it up. She grabs two pints instead of one. She sets the box on the cabinet and walks back into the living room. She sits down on the couch and then the television begins to get blurry and it was then that Neema realized that she was crying. She was fighting an internal battle. She was crying because deep down inside she didn't want to drink. She knows now how easily it could affect others and she no longer wanted to be a part of that. Spending time with Mrs. Stanton today proved that. She was also sad because she couldn't control herself because she felt like she was going to drink no matter what. So, Neema begins to unscrew the top and she drops the top on the floor as if she wouldn't need it again. She starts to bring the bottle up to her lips as tears flowed down her face. Just like before she couldn't stop herself from drinking and she could not control her tears either. Those two helpless thoughts made her cry harder. Once the bottle touched her lips she knew it was useless to fight anymore. Neema stopped resisting and began to do what she does best and that was to drink. She only paused momentarily to catch her breath three times before she finished off the first pint. She looked at the empty bottle and she admired how quickly she finished it. She was once again proud of the way she drinks and that was part of the problem. She took way too much pride in things associated with drinking. That only helped feed her desire to drink often. She holds the bottle up to make sure she had gotten every drop out of it and once she was sure there was nothing left she dropped it on the floor next to the top. Neema turns off the television because it served its purpose as it caused her to drink when she had no intentions too. Besides Neema knew her show was about to go off so she didn't feel like searching through channels to find something else to watch. She got lucky yesterday and found that good black and white movie about the husband and wife. Now she gets a thought about what if she and Dennis was in a television show, what would that be like? Would they be all lovey-dovey or would it be full of drama? That peaked her curiosity so Neema began to think about that. She wondered if their show would be on the Lifetime Network or the OWNed Network. Neema stares at the blank screen on the television as if it was on and she pictured a television episode featuring her and Dennis:

"The Neema and Dennis show"

"Dennis, I have been calling your cell phone. I was wondering what was taking you so long. I was pacing the room, praying that everything was fine. Is everything ok?" *Neema says with a concerned look on her face. She was* worried that something bad had happened to him. She was an extreme worrier and it could be attributed to her anxiety issues she has.

"I am fine Neema. I didn't have my cell phone on me when I went into the store. I was charging the phone with the car charger and I guess I got out of the car and didn't realize that I didn't have it on me. My bad, I should have brought the phone in the store with me." Dennis says as he puts the bag of ice in the sink. He had gone to the store to get ice so they could make daiquiris. The ice, made by their refrigerator, smelled so they never used it. They both wanted daiquiris because that was the drink they had when they first met. Today was their anniversary and they wanted to do things as they always have the past five years.

"I was so scared that something happened because it took you longer than normal since the store is right up the street." Neema says as she opens the bag of ice and puts some ice in the blender.

"It was crowded up there and that was what took so long." Dennis says as he goes to the cabinet to get a couple of glasses.

"Oh ok." Neema says as she starts the blender. She had only needed the ice to be added to the blender because she had already put in the other ingredients. Dennis grabbed the glasses and walked over to Neema nervously. He was worried that Neema was going to ask more probing questions when she was done blending the ice. He knew he had been gone longer than necessary.

"I think that is good." Neema remarks about what she was blending. She removes the top from the blender and waits on Dennis to bring the glasses over. **"It looks real good."**

"Oh yeah, I think you blended it perfectly." Dennis says as he looks into the blender

Neema poured the drink into the glasses.

"Ok, I will bring the glasses out. Can you grab the appetizers?" Neema asks as she takes the glasses from Dennis and motions with her head towards the chips and spinach dip.

"Yeah, I got them." Dennis says as he grabs the chips and spinach dip and follows Neema out to their balcony. They couldn't afford to go out to celebrate so they decided to just have a candle light dinner on their balcony since it had a great view of a large lake. So once they made it to the balcony; they set the drinks, chips and spinach dip down on the table that was already set up out there. Dennis pulls out Neema's chair so she can sit down and *then he walks around to his spot. Neema lit the candles on the table.*

"Ok, the pot roast is almost done so these chips and spinach dip should hold us over until it is finished." *Neema says as she looks at Dennis.*

"Good. I love your pot roast. So let's toast." *Dennis says as he lifts up his drink and waits for Neema to do the same.* **"Let's toast to many more years of happiness and a lifetime of us being together."**

"I will definitely toast to that." *Neema says as they touch glasses and begin to sip on their drinks.* **"I can still remember our first date. I was so nervous that it was hard for me to even speak. I don't remember if I even made eye contact with you that whole night. Just being around you made me so nervous and that was so out of character for me. It was cute though because I knew I liked you."**

"You were nervous? I couldn't even eat. I had saved up that money just to take you out to that expensive restaurant. We both sat there and didn't even touch our food. I knew those plates cost me $50 a piece and we just picked at them. Remember when I asked our waiter for a to-go bag and he told me they didn't have any. That it was customary to eat the food there since it was

against the restaurant's policy to let food be taken out. What restaurant does that kind of mess?" Dennis asks as he shakes his head.

"I know right. I was so shocked but we ate that food though." Neema says as she tries to hold in her laugh.

"You bet we did. We were the last ones to leave but we did it. That was money well spent." Dennis says as he laughs with Neema.

"I am glad it did happen that way because we will never forget that date. I know I never will and it is still as funny today as it was then."

"You know what Neema? It was funny but I was happy because I was with you."

"Aw thank you Dennis. I was glad as well. Now that we have lived through that and we are here. It is so romantic that we are celebrating our first date with the exact same food we had on that night, all the way down to the dessert."

"That is what I am talking about. Neema, you know what I like. That is why I love you so."

Dennis says as he begins to eat some chips and dip.

"That better not be the only reason why you love me?" Neema says as she joins him in eating chips and dip.

"Of course it isn't. I love you for many reasons."

"Tell me some." *Neema asked as she looked into Dennis's eyes.*

"Well, I love you because you are so beautiful, sexy, smart and just a good all-around person. I love everything about you from your smile, to the way you carry yourself and how you always treat me so good. Oh yeah, it is also because I knocked you up." *Dennis says as he tries to hide his smile.*

"What? You are silly. Well if you feel that way then why haven't we been intimate lately?" *Neema asks as her smile is replaced with a serious expression. Dennis knew that this was a common recurring question since Neema had their baby five months ago. Just like all the times before it has caught him totally off guard.*

"Well, I don't know. I just haven't really thought about it."

"Is it because I still haven't lost the weight and I am not a size four anymore?" *Neema asked and she knew it wasn't the best of time to ask him but it has been weighing heavy on her mind.*

*"**Not really.**" Dennis says as he squirms in his seat. Now all of a sudden, the seat he was sitting on wasn't comfortable at all.*

*"**What is it then? You have avoided all of my advances or ignored them. I am feeling like things have changed since before I had the baby. While I was pregnant you didn't want to be intimate. I know I gained weight and all but I still wanted intimacy and it just seemed like you were turned off by me.**" Neema says as she looks Dennis dead in his face. She was looking for any emotional sign from him to show that he was concerned about how she felt.*

*"**Neema, why did you have to bring that up now? We are celebrating our first date. Can you at least wait until the date is over? You don't know what I had planned for later on tonight.**" Dennis says as he tries to hide the fact that he was uncomfortable with her asking him about being intimate. He knew that she couldn't truly handle the truth and so he was going to avoid telling her for however long it took.*

*"**You are right. I did pick a bad time to ask you. It was your idea for this romantic dinner so I should have waited for a better time. I am sorry.**"*

*"**Don't be sorry Neema. Just know that I love you and that won't ever change. I married**"*

you because I love you deeply." Dennis says as he gets up and walks over to Neema. He leans down and kisses her on the lips just to reassure her that he meant what he just said.

"I love you too Dennis. I am happy that we are together and I am happy about this anniversary of our first date. I won't mess up the rest of this night."

"You haven't messed up the night. The night is still young and we have just started. By the end of the night you will have plenty of time to have made it up to me." Dennis says as he winks at Neema and sits down in his chair.

"You are right; I do have plenty of time. I will start by making sure the pot roast is perfect so let me go and check on that and I will be right back. Just continue to enjoy the chips and dip." Neema says as she stands up.

"Better yet, I will just sit here and enjoy the view of you." Dennis says as he looks Neema up and down.

"Whatever." Neema says as she walks back into the apartment. She went to the stove to check on the pot roast. She opened up the stove and she looked in on the pot roast but she couldn't tell if it was done. So she looks around for a pot holder so she could pull the pan out to get a better look. She

sees the pot holder on the counter and she grabs it and picks it up. When she did that, Dennis's keys and change fell on the ground. He had a bad habit of just taking all the contents out of his of pocket and just sitting it on the nearest surface. So he had placed his keys and whatever else that was in his pockets on the kitchen counter and now it was on the floor. So Neema bends over to pick it up and as she picks everything up she notices a small piece of purple paper. Neema picks it up and she looks at it. On the paper was a female's name and number. Neema takes a second look at it and she storms out of the kitchen towards the balcony to confront Dennis.

"Dennis what is this? *Neema says as she walks out unto the balcony. Dennis looked up with a scared but confused look on his face.*

"What is what Sweetheart?" *Dennis asked as Neema walks up to him.*

"What is this? I found this with your keys that were on the counter." *Neema says as she holds the piece of paper out so Dennis can see it but far enough so that he couldn't grab it.*

"Oh that."

"Yeah oh that. I knew something was up when it took you so long to come back from going

a few blocks to get a bag of ice. I felt like you were out there doing something that you shouldn't have been doing and I am right. You were out there getting someone's phone number. That is so low of you to do such a thing. This is our anniversary for crying out loud and you ruined it by going back to your old ways. You are so wrong for this and I will never forgive you."

"Hold on a minute. Are you going to let me talk or what?" *Dennis asks as he stands up so that they are face to face.*

"There is nothing to say. No excuse for why you were out there getting some woman's phone number on our special night."

"Neema please let me explain."

"For what? I have heard all the excuses before and none of them are good enough to explain why you have this number right here. You know what you can eat the pot roast and cheesecake by yourself. I am going to bed because I don't want to talk to you right now." *Neema says as she turns around and walks back into the house. Dennis follows her as he is trying to get her attention.*

"Neema I wasn't trying to get anyone's phone number. You have to believe me."

*"**Just like I should have believed you the first time it happened or the second time. Well, this is time number six and so I guess I should just be forgiving of you again? How many times is too many times Dennis?"** Neema asked without even turning around. She just kept on walking through the kitchen and down the hall that led to their bedroom. Dennis was close on her heels.*

*"**Sweetheart, please listen to me. There is a simple explanation about the number."** Dennis says as he wants to plead his case.*

*"**I bet there is Dennis, I bet there is."** Neema says as she sits down on their bed.*

*"**Neema there is a simple explanation for it. That piece of paper just flew into my pocket."***

Neema gives Dennis a look of "Are you serious." She looks at the name and number again and looks up at Dennis.

*"**Nice try. This is Miss Baltimore's name and number. She is the church tramp that you have been seeing behind my back."** Neema says matter-of-factly.*

*"**She is not a tramp, she is just free with her body. Her gift to men is to share her body with whoever needs it. She is very caring that way."** Dennis says as he sits on the bed next to Neema*

and puts his arm around her shoulders. Neema knocked his arm away and looked at him with a look that could have burnt a hole through his soul.

"Wow. I am sorry Dennis. I didn't realize she was that nice to let men have her body like that. Who am I to look down on her for being so nice to so many men, including married ones?" *Neema says as she shakes her head in disbelief that Dennis would even take up for Miss Baltimore.*

"Don't worry about it. I had no plans on calling her tonight. I was going to wait until you visit your mom on the weekend. She told me that she didn't want to be selfish and take precious quality time away from me and you. It is so amazing how considerate Miss Baltimore is of your feelings. She is such a sweetheart." *Dennis says as he speaks glowingly of Miss Baltimore.*

"Oh I love that about her too as well. I can't wait until I see her again so I can tell her how much I appreciate her sweetness." *Neema says being sarcastic. She has some words for Miss Baltimore but none was appreciation.*

"Oh she would love that. She loves being thanked for what she has done. Whenever men thank her for a great time she always tears up and gets emotional." *Dennis says with seriousness in his voice. Neema wanted to punch him dead in his* *face for being so stupid to think she cared anything about Miss. Baltimore's feelings. She is sleeping with the whole city and Dennis thinks she deserves a medal of honor for sharing her body with all the men she can.*

"Ok." *Neema says as she grabs Dennis's hand as they walk out of the bedroom and into the kitchen. Neema winks at Dennis as she grabs a large kitchen knife. He sees her do that and he wonders why.*

"Neema what is that for?" *Dennis asked.*

"Oh this is practice for me. I am going to cut you to the white meat and then I am going to cut her into small pieces and bury her in a shallow grave." *Neema says as she stares at Dennis.*

"No don't be that way. Let's just refocus on this wonderful meal prepared by my wonderful wife." *Dennis says as he smiles at Neema.*

"Are you crazy!!!!!? You just said the dumbest thing in the whole wide world to me. You want me to cosign on you sleeping with Miss Baltimore and pretend like that is normal and sit here and enjoy this meal. You are out of this world crazy." *Neema says as she has just about had enough of the foolishness that is coming out of Dennis's mouth.*

*"**How did you know I wasn't from this world?**" Dennis says as his skin turns green and eyes turn yellow and he becomes an alien.*

*"**My momma was right about you.**" Neema says as she stands up with the knife in her hand ready to fight Dennis who is now an alien.*

The end

This episode was brought you by Crown Royal.

Neema bursts out laughing at what she just thought of. She knows that show won't be on the Lifetime Network but the SYFY one instead. She couldn't help but laugh at the turn of events in the show. Thinking about it and the way it turned out makes her wonder. Is Miss Baltimore trying to steal Dennis from her? Neema knows that Miss Baltimore better back up or she will catch these hands.

"Woman I will beat you silly. Leave my man alone." Neema says as if she is talking to Miss Baltimore. She is pointing and moving her head and neck for emphasis.

"I will run your skinny tail over, I have done it before, and I will do it again." Neema says as she grabs the other bottle and began to drink from it when she hears a knock at the front door. Neema stopped drinking to answer the door.

"Who is it?" Neema yelled.

"It's me Torii."

Neema opened the door and she was happy at first but then she remembered what happened at church on Sunday and her smile quickly went away and she didn't care if Torii noticed.

"Hey Torii."

"Neema!" Torii says as she steps in and gives Neema a hug and for a moment Neema felt better.

"Come on in." Neema says as she closes the front door. Torii followed her into the living room and sat down next to her.

"What you doing Neema?" Torii asked in her childlike fashion.

"I have been relaxing and drinking." Neema says as she grabs her pint of Crown Royal.

"I thought you didn't drink?"

"I do on occasions. It makes me feel good inside." Neema says as she forgot she told Torii and Dennis that she hates alcohol and doesn't drink but that one time she got her DWI.

"Can I taste some? My friend at school says his brother gives him some on the weekends. His brother told him it will put hair on his chest one day." Torii asked as she looked at the bottle in Neema's hand.

"You want hair on your chest?" Neema asks as she laughs at the thought of that.

"No not really but I do want to taste it. I am curious."

"Don't be because it is bad for you. It will make you do things you don't want to do." Neema says as she takes a swig of it.

"My mom use to give me a spoon full of her wine sometimes."

"You for real?" Neema asked.

"She did, but I never told my dad because he would get mad."

"You were smart to not tell him because you would get in big trouble I am sure. Not that I care though because you and your father lied to me yesterday. You didn't even come over to hang with me." Neema says as she looks at Torii with the side-eye.

"I did come over. I knocked and knocked but you didn't answer. We saw your car so we figured you were home."

"What? I didn't hear you knocking." Neema says as she tries to remember it but she couldn't.

"I did, twice."

"What time was it?" Neema asked.

"It was 5:00pm."

"That sure was a long time after you guys ate. Dennis told me that you were coming back right after you were done eating. Instead he wanted to hang out with Miss Baltimore."

"No we didn't. My dad figured he would give you more time to finish your work so we went shopping and hung out until he figured you would be free. That's why we were late." Torii says with her innocent voice.

"Oh." Neema says as she begins to feel better about the situation than she did yesterday. She was acting all jealous yesterday for nothing and she didn't know all the facts.

"Oh, can I watch television, I think my favorite show is on." Torii asks as her alarm went off on her cell phone. Neema hands her the remote.

"Where is your father at now?" Neema asked.

"He is at home doing laundry because he does it every Monday." Torii says as she finds her show on the television. Neema takes a few more swigs and she sets the bottle down on the table.

"Okay, I need to go talk to him right quick. You stay here and I will be right back."

"Okay, I will just watch my show."

"Yeah watch all you want." Neema says as she goes to her purse and she grabs a couple sticks of gum and begin to chew it to hopefully mask the alcohol that was on her breath. She wanted to talk to Dennis one on one about the feelings she has for him.

"Be right back Torii." Neema says as she walks out the door and closes it behind her. She begins to walk to Torii's house when suddenly it feels like she is on a ship at sea because she began to rock from side to side. It felt like the whole earth was moving under her feet. The door was about twenty feet ahead but with every step she took it seemed to move farther away. Neema couldn't really stay focused on the distance of the door because she was too busy trying to walk in a straight line. She eventually came to her senses and used the wall as a guide and walked along side of it. She made it to Torii's house and she knocked on the door. She couldn't decide on how she was going to greet Dennis. She didn't know if she should give him a hug or a handshake. Better yet, should she give him a kiss like they do in the movies? While she was standing there thinking about what she was going to do, Dennis had already opened the door.

"Neema."

"Oh hey Dennis." Neema says as she snaps out of her daze.

"I thought Torii was over at your place?" Dennis asked.

"She is, but I just wanted to talk to you about something." Neema says feeling bold and confident.

"Did Torii do something wrong?" Dennis asked sounding like a parent that knows their children are bound to mess up.

"No, she is perfect. She is watching television at my place."

"Okay well come in." Dennis says as he opens the door wider so Neema could come inside. Neema's foot hit the lip of the doorway and she stumbles into the apartment.

"Hey, are you okay?" Dennis asked as he grabs Neema because her clumsiness has caught him off guard.

"I am fine. These are new shoes and I haven't broken them in yet." Neema says as she plays it off. She had to because it wasn't clumsiness that caused her to trip but alcohol.

"Okay let's have a seat on the couch. Would you like something to drink?" Dennis asked as he walked into the kitchen. Neema just stared at him like he was a well-cooked steak on a dinner plate.

"No thank you." Neema replies as she attempts to walk to the living room. This was her first time inside of Torii's apartment so she was taking in the sights as she was looking around at the decor. She knows that all the floor plans of every apartment are different so if she had not been drunk she would have seen that she was about to miss a step as she steps into the living room. As if on cue, she doesn't notice the step and when she stepped down, over the step, her body was confused on where the ground went. The drop was enough to cause her to fall off balance and the alcohol in her system only aided her clumsiness and she fell like she had been shot by a sniper's rifle. Neema crashes onto a small end table that was at the end of the couch. On top of the end table was a clear vase that had flowers in it and when Neema crashed on top of the end table the vase fell to the floor and smashed into many pieces. Not to be out done, Neema's momentum caused her to flip over the end table and she lands on the hardwood floor as well and together with the sound of the vase breaking only enhanced the commotion she was causing. Dennis heard the vase break and he came running into the living room.

"What? Neema are you okay? What happened?" Dennis asked as he runs up to Neema. He notices the vase smashed on the floor and Neema laying sprawled on the floor.

"I tripped over the step coming into the living room." Neema says as she points to the step she missed.

"Are you alright? Can you get up?" Dennis asked.

"Yes I can." Neema says as she begins to stand up. Dennis helps her up to her feet and Neema nodded to let him know she was okay.

"Okay I am going to get a broom and dustpan to get this broken vase up." Dennis says as he walks out the living room.

"Okay, I am going to sit down." Neema says as she takes a step towards the couch but for some reason her body began to lean towards the flat screen television that was on a large stand with Dennis's DVD player, Xbox and CD\DVDs. Neema tried to fight the pull of her body but it was impossible to stop herself from moving towards it. Dennis comes in just in time because he seen Neema stumbling towards the television and he dropped the broom and dustpan and caught her right before she crashed into the television.

"Neema, did you hit your head or something?" Dennis asked with concern in his voice as he stared into Neema's eyes.

"No, I don't know what's up. I think your floor is slanted or something." Neema says as Dennis makes a strange face and she realized that she had seen that expression before. She tries to remember where she had seen it and then it comes to her. It was the same look the paramedic gave her at the scene of the accident.

"Neema, have you been drinking?" Dennis asked as he shakes his head in disproval to whatever the answer was going to be. Neema didn't like the look and she wanted to tell him no because that confused look he had would most certainly turn into a disappointed one. Neema had every intention to lie to Dennis. She doesn't care about what he witnessed or what his suspicions are. Neema was going to tell him no she hadn't been drinking but just like with the policeman at the accident, her mouth was more than happy to brag about what she had been doing.

"Yes I have." Neema answers rather confidently and Dennis's face went from confused to disgusted in half a second. Dennis walks away from Neema and grabs the broom and dustpan and begins to get up the broken vase. He walks into the kitchen and comes back with a towel to dry up the water that was left. Neema watched him take care of her mess she created and she felt the way she felt with Mrs. Stanton when she was ignoring Neema in the car. Neema tried to take a step towards Dennis but she felt unstable as the room begin to start spinning so she thought better of it.

"I thought you were better than that, Neema. I don't understand why you let yourself get this drunk." Dennis says with a disappointed look on his face.

"I am not drunk, I was just off balance." Neema says as she tries to convince Dennis that she was okay.

"Please, you can barely stand up straight and I doubt you can walk in a straight line."

"Dennis shut up. I can do more than just walk in a straight line. I can turn around in a circle and walk ten straight lines." Neema says as she begins to turn in a circle in place and that set her equilibrium in motion so as soon as she stopped and tried to take a step, her body began to pull her backwards and she stumbled into the wall behind her, knocking down pictures that were hung on it. Neema slid down the wall like they do in the cartoons when they run into a wall and she slid down to her butt. Dennis had a look on his face like he was upset but Neema didn't understand why.

"Why are you looking at me like that? You didn't just fall down, I did. Why did you put this wall right here?" Neema asks as she is confused on why the wall caused her to fall.

"What? Are you serious? I can't believe you are this wasted right now."

"I am not wasted, I am just buzzing." Neema says as she tries to get up but her body wasn't cooperating.

"Get up." Dennis says with anger in his voice.

"I would if your floor would stop tripping. It won't let me get up. Tell your floor to stop." Neema says as she tries to stand up again but her balance is gone.

"Let me help you up so you can go home." Dennis says as he walks up to Neema and helps her to her feet. When Dennis had her fully standing up, Neema tried to lean in to kiss him but Dennis backed away from her.

"Thanks Big Dennis. You are so strong. Pick me up again." Neema says as she stretches her arms out to Dennis but he pushed them away.

"I totally shocked right now. I would have never thought you had a drinking problem but I should have known. I have the same things in my step father, who was an alcoholic and me and my mom had to suffer abuse behind him. I made a promise that alcohol would never play a role in my life again because there is no safety in being around someone who has a problem with drinking. I have seen the first hand effects of drinking and it always starts off small but it just progresses to something that can't be controlled. I don't know what point you are at but I know something is wrong. To think I let my daughter hang around you and you might have a problem with drinking. Now it all makes sense because you were drunk at your accident and that should have thrown up a red flag. That was one of the reasons why Torii hasn't been over to your apartment that much because I tried to see how this was going to play out. I needed to know if that was a one-time accident but what I see today assures me of my worst fears. I think you might have a drinking problem." Dennis says as he grabs the towel and quickly walks into the kitchen so he won't drip water everywhere. Neema just stood there like a statue because she didn't know exactly what to say. She felt he was right because she does have a drinking problem. It was a problem that she had no control over. Neema realized that today now that others have shed light on her issues that can't be ignored. It was clearer than ever that she has a serious problem that needs to be addressed. So as Dennis was returning from the kitchen, Neema wanted to talk about the reason why she came over and that was to talk about the feelings she has for him but she thought better of it and didn't mention it.

"Dennis, I am so sorry. I do have a problem and you are not the first person to tell me so. I realize that now and I see that I do need help. I just don't know where to go or what to do."

"Why is that so easy for someone to say? My step father said the same thing as my mom set him up with appointment after appointment. Every time he left the house we were under the assumption that he was going to appointments but he was somewhere getting drunk. You are a grown woman, Neema. You are trying to tell me you have no clue as to where you could find help? You could find that alcohol you were drinking with no problem though. I feel sorry for you but you will get no sympathy from me because sympathy doesn't work with addictions. No you need someone to put their foot down and hopefully it will force you to get something done." Dennis say as he just stares at Neema and she could see the frustrated look on his face.

"Dennis I don't know what else to say. Well, can you help me find the help I need?" Neema asked.

"I am sorry Neema but I won't help you. If you were truly serious about helping yourself, then you would take the effort to find the right place for you. One thing about addictions is the fact that the person feels they are dependent on the substance and they can't do anything else. You are not going to depend on me to help you fight your addiction. You need to draw on the strength that you have within you to do that. I refuse to get hurt by expecting you to do what is necessary after I have taken the time and effort to set everything up for you. I told myself to never again be put in that situation. Even though you mean a lot to me, I won't be your crutch. That is the last thing you need is a crutch when you are trying to get rid of the crutch you already have." Dennis says as what he is saying is hitting Neema like a ton of bricks. This day has turned into an eye opening experience for Neema. Ever since she first woke up this morning, everything she has done has been a challenge. A challenge that has tested her physically and mentally. She thought her quick fixes she was using would be able to get her through the issues but the reality was they were only covering up the problems. At the end of it all the problem was still there awaiting to be addressed. This was a day that Neema wanted to forget because she has caused more pain than anything else. Suddenly the front door opens and it is Torii. She was holding her head and was off balanced as she walked into the apartment.

"Daddy." Torii says as she sits on the floor in the entrance of her apartment with the door wide open behind her. Neema stood there glued to the spot she was standing in. It was as if she was watching everything transpire on a television show.

"What's wrong baby?" Dennis asks as he runs up to Torii.

"I don't feel good." Torii says as she begins to cry.

"Is it your head? Your stomach? What baby? Tell me what's hurting." Dennis says as he looks at Torii face to see if he could tell what was wrong with her.

"I think I am going to be sick." Torii says as she begins to stand up.

"Hurry, let's go to the bathroom. Try to hold it in until we get there." Dennis says as he helps guide Torii to the bathroom. Neema stood there as if this was the commercial break in the television show she was watching. She was just going to stand there until they came back into view. She had mixed emotions about the whole situation. She didn't know what was wrong with Torii and at the same time she wouldn't be able to help her in the state she was in. Neema knew she couldn't even take a step without losing her balance so what good would she be to Torii right now.

"I know that is not what I smell." Neema hears Dennis say as she hears every step he takes as he is walking back to the living room. The look on his face said it all.

"Neema, leave my house right now before I call the police on you." Dennis says as he points at the front door. Neema was shocked because she didn't know what was going on.

"What did I do?" Neema asked with a puzzled look on her face.

"What do you mean? You know what you did." Dennis says with a stern look on his face.

"I have no clue what you are talking about." Neema pleads with Dennis to let him know she needed more information from him.

"You want to play dumb, okay. You can listen as I call the police to tell them what you did." Dennis says as he pulls out his cell phone from his pocket. Neema's heart starts to beat faster than ever before because all she could think about was going to jail. She was told by the judge not to drink and this is violating court orders. If the police show up, she was looking at ten years in jail.

"Wait Dennis. I am serious. I don't know what you are talking about. Please tell me what I did wrong." Neema pleads as she was scared beyond measure.

"You can try to play me for a fool if you want to but I know you know what I am talking about. Just for the sake of arguing I am going to tell you. You know you can't deny the fact that you gave Torii some alcohol. I smelled it as she was throwing up."

What Dennis said hit Neema right in the heart. Neema knew she didn't give Torii any alcohol. As a matter of fact, if Torii was old enough to drink, Neema still wouldn't have shared her stash with her. Neema remembers not giving her any before she left.

"What are you talking about? I would never give Torii alcohol."

"How did she get it then? She was over your house. I don't have any over here. Since you are clearly drunk, you probably don't even remember if you gave it to her or not. Whatever the case may be, you need to leave because I still have a good mind to call the police. By the way, Torii will never go back over to your apartment and do me a favor and leave us alone." Dennis says with a look on his face that Neema never wants to see again and she knows he was dead serious. Neema was crushed because Torii did mean a lot to her. Tears began to form in her eyes as she realizes the relationship with Torii and the friendship with Dennis was over. Neema knew that her feelings she had for Dennis meant nothing now and even if she confessed them it wouldn't make a difference right now.

"I am so sorry Dennis." Neema says as she wipes the tears off of her face.

"Sorry just doesn't cut it. Torii could have died because of you. I am dead serious when I say I want you out of my apartment now." Dennis says as he walks towards the front door. Neema begins to follow him and it was still a battle to get her body to function normally. As she approached the step in the living room that started all the drama, Neema had it in her mind to pick her leg up high enough to avoid it but she ends up clipping it with her foot and begins to stumble towards the front door. Dennis just watched as Neema regained her balance as she held on to the wall for dear life. Neema knew she needed to say something. She just couldn't let this situation end their friendship they had. Neema didn't want to lose Torii or Dennis for that fact. She wanted to stay a part of their life so she tried to think of something to say before she left. She didn't know what to say but she still looked Dennis in the face and she saw the anger and she knew she had caused it. Her mind went blank as she opened her mouth to say one last thing to help her case. So, Neema blurted out the first thing that came to her mind.

"Ephesians 5:18."

Neema was shocked by what she had just said. She remembered reading that on the sign that was above the spot where she hit Mrs. Stanton. She still didn't have any clue as to why she said it or what it meant. It was a mystery as to why that came out of her mouth so she just politely walked away and left Torii's apartment. Neema stumble back to her apartment and she noticed that Torii had left the front door wide open. Neema walked in and slammed the door behind her. She went in the living room and she seen the bottle that she had set on the table was lower than when she left. Torii had took a few drinks of it and Neema knew it was her fault. She shouldn't have been drinking in front of Torii. She could have put the alcohol up until Torii had left and that would have been the responsible thing to do. Now she was mad at herself for not doing the responsible thing then but she knows the responsible thing to do now. She grabs the bottle off the table and the one that was on the floor. She takes them into the kitchen and sets them on the cabinet by the sink. She looked at the sink and she knows what she must do but her arms wouldn't pick the bottles up so she could pour it into the sink. It was as if her body was trying to stop her from getting rid of the alcohol.

"Neema do it, now." Neema says as she begins to cry and she picks up the pint of Crown Royal and she holds it over the sink. Her hands were shaking as she slowly poured out the alcohol into the sink. Neema was so upset that she was crying over some alcohol and now she is beginning to see how far gone she is with drinking. She puts the two empty bottles in the trash. She opens the box she left on the cabinet that had the last pint of Crown Royal left. She grabs it and without hesitation she unscrews the top and pours the contents into the sink. This was the first time that she has ever treated alcohol with contempt. She had never had the strength to pour out alcohol in the past but after today she was ready to make a change. Everything that took place today happened because of the alcohol and there was no denying that. Neema felt like she has had enough. She wished Dennis believed that as well because she could use him in her corner. The strength she would gain from having him there would be more than enough to help her but Dennis didn't want to have anything to do with her. Neema found herself crying harder because she knows she never told Dennis how she felt and she wished that was the last thing she had told him. Instead the last thing she said to Dennis was something she had no clue about. Neema waits until the last drop was gone from the bottle before she chunks it and the box it was in into the trash. She then walks to her bedroom and goes to her closet. She looks on the top shelf and she sees the black box that her parents gave her when she moved out. She grabs it and removes the lid and the first thing she sees is a Bible. She grabs the Bible and she sits on her bed. She opens it up and she looks in the table of contents for Ephesians because this was her first time in a long time opening a Bible. She found the page number and flips over to it. She skims down the page until she comes to the verse she was looking up and she read it out loud.

"And be not drunk with wine, wherein is excess; but be filled with the Spirit."

Neema says as she reads it again. She was trying to figure out the meaning. She knows the first part that basically speaks upon not drinking until you are drunk. The second part was talking about being filled with the Holy Spirit and she knows she hasn't acted like she was filled with the Holy Spirit in years. She wasn't a frequent visitor to church but she is not dumb. She knows that she gave her life to God in high school but never took it serious and here she is today needing God more than ever. She knows she is buzzing but she found herself falling to her knees and crying her heart out. Neema began to apologize to God and to tell him everything she should have said years ago. Now she feels like she has let God down. After she was done bearing her soul Neema began to try to put the pieces together. Neema can understand why they put the sign above the spot where she hit Mrs.

Stanton but she wanted to know more about the verse. So, Neema begins to read the whole book of Ephesians in hope of shedding more light into the verse.

Chapter Four

"Neema. Mr. Derby would like to see you in his office." The receptionist says over the intercom. The sound of her voice snapped Neema out of her daze. It has been a month since her last drink on the day her life came to a halt. She was towing the line between jail and freedom. She ruined a relationship with Torii and Dennis and that was the final straw. Not almost being sentenced to ten years in prison, or almost killing someone. No the simplest thing she lost was the dearest to her heart. Neema was just thinking about how a lot has happened since that fateful night she stopped drinking cold turkey. The first couple of days were unbearable because she couldn't even sleep. She tossed and turned as her body was upset at the fact that she wouldn't give in to the thirst. Not even when the migraine headaches came or the constant stomach ache that had her doubled over in pain. She didn't give up when she had the sweats or was always irritable. When Neema was at her breaking point she had to check herself into a hospital because she was at her wits end. It was there they connected her to an AA chapter that was near her home. She went to her first meeting two weeks ago. It went better than she expected and she was more than happy to join the program. It made her feel real good to seek help. She was honest with them and with everyone else that she was close to. Mr. Derby has been great because he holds her accountable and has been the one to attend a meeting with Neema to keep her motivated. Neema even noticed a change in Mrs. Stanton since she told her that she was seeking help for her drinking problem. The bitterness has been dialed down from a ten to an eight but it was a start. So, even though this was only the beginning, she still felt like she was making progress in the right direction. So, she gets up and walks out of her office to head to Mr. Derby's office. Once she rounds the corner she can see that Mr. Derby is not alone in his office. There were two men that were part of the investor team sitting in his office with him. One was a rather large man that was wearing an expensive pinstriped suit. He had some blond curly hair that accented his red cheeks that reminded her of Santa Claus. He had on some eyeglasses that were large but sporty. He was barely able to fit into the chair that he was sitting in. The other gentlemen was scrawny with a terrible comb over. It was too noticeable but if it worked for him then more power to him. He was wearing a black suit in the skinny jean style as it hugged his thin frame. These were two of the bigger investors because Neema remembers Mr. Derby calling them Laurel and Hardy.

"Neema, come on in." Mr. Derby says as he flashes that smile that let Neema know that he had some good news. Neema steps in the door and she sees a chair that was empty between the two investors. Neema walks up shakes the investor's hands and takes her seat in between them.

"Well Neema, I have called you in because there are some things that we need to talk about. Don't be nervous because everything is great." Mr. Derby says as he sees the uneasy look on Neema's face. Neema thought she was hiding it but obviously she wasn't doing a good job of it. So Neema took a deep breath, sat back and relaxed.

"Mr. Longley and Mr. Jacobs came all the way from New York to tell you some good news. Fellas, the floor is yours." Mr. Derby says as he nods at the two investors. They both looked at each other as if to say, "You go first." The heavyset guy holds up his hand to begin to speak first.

"Miss Smart, we came down here to share a bit of good news with you. It has been an extremely long time since the last time we have done this. We, Mr. Longley and I, want to be the first to tell you how well your idea is taking off. We have made major strides on the East coast and I will tell you that you couldn't have picked a better time to launch your idea." Mr. Jacobs says as he smiles.

"Indeed. We unleashed this new idea during the beginning of the election year and you better believe that they have been popping up everywhere. All over the cities everyone has something to say and they are using your idea as an avenue to get their word out." Mr. Longley says as he starts to get excited.

"That is just the tip of the iceberg. I don't know if Mr. Derby has mentioned to you but we have a large sales conference coming up next week. We want you there so you can better explain your ideas to areas we haven't reached like up North and Northwest regions of the United States. I feel with the numbers we have put up on the East coast, you could easily get the sales force to get aboard." Mr. Jacobs says as he taps Neema's arm in excitement.

"Not only that but we are going to make the deal sweeter. We want to offer you a new position. A position that will basically oversee all the products within the urban areas and you will get a commission on each sign that is put up."

"This a great opportunity for you because we know you have great potential. Let's not slow down the momentum you have achieved. We have talked things over with Mr. Derby so take look over the contract we have drafted up and let us know.

Mr. Jacobs says as he shakes Neema's hand and Mr. Longley does the same.

"Mr. Derby, "Sit in the back" taxi service is here. The receptionist says over the intercom.

"Thank you Linda. Fellas that is your chariot. We appreciate you coming and giving us such good news. Have a safe trip back and we will be in contact with you in a few days.

"No, thank you Mr. Derby." Mr. Longley says as Mr. Jacobs nods his head in agreement. The two investors walked out of Mr. Derby's office and he closes the door behind them. He walks back over to his desk and sits down.

"So, what do you think?" Mr. Derby asked.

"I am a little overwhelmed by all of this."

"Neema, I don't see why. Anytime you have an idea you should always prepare like it is going to be the next big thing. If not, then you are selling your idea short and that leads to doubt. This is about to take off so fast that it will make your head spin."

"Mr. Derby, I feel it spinning already." Neema says as she begins to get excited by what is taking place. She can still remember a few months ago when she brought her idea in front of the investors. There was so much doubt there that she felt like her idea was dumb. Mr. Derby felt otherwise and he kept on telling her that she was on to something special and now she can see it as well.

"Well get ready to be dizzy because you will definitely have the potential to make six figures a year. Just think about bringing home that type of money."

"That is a lot of money. What do I need to do?" Neema asked.

"First you must accept the offer. Next you will go to the convention next week and then prepare yourself to do a lot of traveling as you will have to go to different sale's meetings coast to coast." Mr. Derby says as he tells her what her next course of action is.

"A lot of traveling?" Neema asked.

"Yes. That might be the only drawback about it. I know you have the thing with Mrs. Stanton twice a week. Is there any way that someone else could fill in for you?"

"I don't think so because it was the court's orders. I won't be able to be free from that portion of the sentencing until Mrs. Stanton can freely walk again.

"I do understand. Let's see if we can work something out so you won't miss the days of rehab with Mrs. Stanton. I don't want to mess with what the court says because they were lenient enough in the first place."

"That is so true. They were real lenient with me and I don't want to rock the boat."

"I am telling you Neema, these investors are sold on your ideas. They know a cash cow when they see it. I went out and took some pictures of some of the existing signs that we have throughout this city. Let me tell you their eyes lit up like a cake for a one hundred year old person. Here take a look at these photos." Mr. Derby says as he hands Neema a brown envelope. Neema takes the envelope and begins to look through the pictures. She recognized the majority of the signs that she has seen as she drove around Houston. She notices the one at the spot where she hit Mrs. Stanton.

"That was the one that sold them. Those inventors saw that Bible verse and they were set off like a firework show." Mr. Derby says as he claps his hands. He was feeling a different type of emotion than Neema was. Neema felt sadness but relief because of what took place there has changed her life for the better. That sign has given her the strength to stop drinking so just like this picture meant a lot to the investors, it means a whole lot more to Neema.

"Great pictures and just looking at them, gets me more excited to see all the different ways people are using them." Neema says as she gets chills thinking about this was her idea.

"We have a few days to work on what we should say so you can have your rehab days free. I don't want to tell them about it was court's orders because they don't need to know about that night or what you are currently going through. I will help you conceal that so don't you worry. Now go ahead and look over the contract. I forwarded it to your email." Mr. Derby says as he takes the pictures from Neema.

"Thank you Mr. Derby." Neema says as she walks out of the office. Everything sounded so good and she was all set for making more money especially since she is paying for Mrs. Stanton's rehab. A pay raise and an appreciation for her idea has put Neema into a state of happiness that she has longed for.

Neema pulled into her assigned parking spot in front of her apartment. She has been on cloud nine since she left the office. It was funny because she had missed her exit, because out of a force of habit, she actually took the exit that takes her to her favorite liquor store. As soon as she realized her mistake, she quickly turned around and came straight home. Her mind almost wrote a check that her body can't cash. Neema actually enjoyed being sober and she felt better about gaining self-control. There are still the headaches she gets and the desire is still as strong as ever but she is determined to beat this addiction. Neema knows the best strategy is one day at a time. She congratulates herself every morning and night that she stays sober. It is just a reminder that every moment of sobriety should be celebrated. As soon as she put her car in park, she looked through her windshield and she saw Torii standing near her apartment. Neema's heart begin to beat fast because this is the first time she has made eye contact with Torii since that day a month ago. As soon as Neema opened her car door, Torii took off running in the direction of her apartment. That really disappointed Neema but she figured Dennis told her to not speak or go near Neema. She has to respect his wishes as a father and she doesn't want to get Torii in trouble. Neema wished she would have waved at Torii at least but that would have made matters worse. Neema walks down the sidewalk to get to her apartment and she sees that familiar bike laying in the middle of the sidewalk. The one she tripped and fell on. As a matter of fact, that bike is always there. Whoever owns it never lays it in the grass but leaves it right in the middle of the sidewalk. This time Neema easily steps over the bike and she smiled because it was her inside joke since no one seen her fall on it last time. So she continues to walk to her apartment because she was hungry and she wanted to try this new recipe. She walks into her apartment and walks straight to the kitchen so she could take out everything she needs for the recipe. Suddenly there was a knock on the front door. Neema goes to answer it.

"Who is it?" Neema asked.

"It's Torii."

Neema knew she shouldn't be here so her plan was to tell her to go home. Neema opened the door and she sees Torii and Dennis standing there. Torii steps up and gives Neema a big hug. Neema didn't know what to do so she hugged her back as she fought back tears.

"Hey Neema." Dennis says as he smiles.

"Hey Dennis." Neema says as she is totally confused on why they came over her house. He made it plain as day that he didn't want them to ever talk again but here they are.

"I missed you Neema." Torii says as she continues to hug Neema.

"What's up Torii?" Neema says as she enjoys the big hug Torii was giving her.

"May we come in and talk?" Dennis asked as he watch Torii give Neema the longest hug ever.

"Yes come on in." Neema says as she still doesn't know what is going on but she is happy that she was able to enjoy a hug from Torii. She leads them into her living room and they all sit down on the couch.

"Okay, I want to apologize first of all. I had no right to belittle you about your drinking habits. I didn't know what you were going through at the time. I was out of line to compare you to my step father who was the worst of the worst. I overreacted to everything that took place that night. When Torii came home sick and I smelled the alcohol, I assumed that you gave it to her. Torii told me you didn't give her any alcohol. She said she took it upon herself to drink some after you left. She said you told her never to drink but her curiosity got the best of her. I just want to apologize for treating you terribly and kicking you out of my life for a misunderstanding." Dennis says as he looks at Neema with a humbled look on his face. Neema was happy that he apologized but she felt he didn't need to.

"I want to say that I am sorry too. I played a major role in what took place last week. I was out of line to drink in front of Torii in the first place. That was definitely the wrong example to set because look what happened because of it. I am guilty as charged for her drinking alcohol for I was the one that left it out so she had access to it. I should have put it away but no I left it right next to her and that was stupid on my part. It doesn't matter that I told her not to drink it, I should have been the responsible adult in that situation. I also feel you were not out of line to fuss at me because of what happened to Torii. I wouldn't expect you to act any differently. Only a parent that truly loves their child would take their child's well-being over a friendship. I know Torii means the world to you and you would protect her at all costs. I love Torii also and I would want you to act exactly the way you did. So I am sorry for what happened to Torii,

your table, your vase and what happened to us."
Neema says as she looks at Dennis to see what his
reaction was to what she just said because she was
trying to be funny.

"What concerned me too is your
relationship with Torii. I spoke to her and she was
hurt when I told her she couldn't talk to you
anymore. She was crying off and on for about a
week. So, I sat her down and we had a major heart
to heart talk. The things she said about you are the
things she said about her mom and I know how
much she loved her. It moved me to know that she
was attached to you more than she was attached
to my sister or any other female family member. I
had been longing for her to have a female in her
life that she could latch on to and have a bond that
will help her as she gets older. She told me that you
were the one she looked up to the most and so I
knew what I needed to do. I swallowed my pride
and I decided that we need to bury the hatchet and
make things right. Besides, I had some feelings
going on that I didn't know I had." Dennis says as
he looks away as if he was trying to hide what his
eyes were trying to say.

Neema felt that this was a great time to tell Dennis
what was on her heart. In the past she had given all
her emotions to her drinking problem. That was
what took up the majority of her time and she had

no room for anything else. Now that she is sober, with a clear mind, she realizes that she has missed out on so much and Neema knows that needs to end today.

"Dennis I need to tell you something. As a matter of fact, I was going to tell you this before I decided to play tackle football with your table and vase in your living room." Dennis laughs at the sound of that and Neema knew she needed that to break the tension in the room.

"Anyway, I came over there to tell you how I truly felt about you. At first I thought maybe it was just the alcohol making me feel that way. I had been getting drunk basically every day so I couldn't tell if it was my feelings or the alcohol. Well, I haven't had a drink in a month and you are still on my mind. Day and night I think of what could have been. I think of spending time together talking, enjoying dinners and getting to know each other on a deeper level. I have truly missed Torii and our interactions together and I must say that was one of the motivating factors in me getting cleaned up and changing my life. You don't know this but I am in a local AA chapter near here so I can continue to get the help I need so I can be better for myself. I say all of this to not bombard you with my feelings to paint you in a corner so you have to make any decisions. I am telling you this because I have feelings for you. I don't care if you feel the same way or not because I will be there for Torii no matter what so there is no pressure on you at all. I just want to be a part of Torii's life." Neema says as she begins to feel so much better that she has finally got that off her chest. It was hurting her, on the inside, that she couldn't express her feelings.

"Neema, I don't know what to say. I have wanted to tell you how I felt for the longest but I was afraid to. We have different lives and I didn't see any common ground except for Torii. I didn't want to put her in the middle because if we had a relationship together and it failed, she would be the one to lose. I can't stand to see her emotionally suffering because of something I did so I never mentioned how I felt to you because I did not want to run you away. I didn't want you to feel trapped by me by using Torii as way to ensnare you in a relationship. I was clueless what to do so I just kept my feelings locked up inside. I also want to be honest with you. Another reason why I never approached you was because of my faith in Christ. I really don't know where you are in your walk but I was afraid that we are unequally yoked. I am not trying to judge you at all but I am only making an observation about what I have seen from you and believe me I am not trying to disrespect you." Dennis says as nicely as he could put it.

"No you didn't disrespect me. I know exactly what you mean and you are right. My walk with God is pretty much nonexistent. I know all about God but I chose to stay away from the church because of my drinking issue. I didn't want to sit in church and hear about my faults because I wanted to just ignore them and deal with them through the bottle. I love me some Jesus because of what he has done for me, but I have let life cloud my ability to show the world that."

"Well that is good to know then because I have been surrounding myself with people that want to walk this walk with me. I have dated in the past and if they weren't trying to grow spiritually the relationship stalled every time. I just want to bring the right someone into Torii's life that will be able to show her how to bring God glory through her life as a woman and that is something I can't do."

"If you don't mind I do want to start going to church with you. I don't want to make Miss Baltimore mad if I do start going." Neema says as she tries to see what that relationship was about.

"Don't worry about Miss Baltimore, she is just a friend who likes to talk a lot. She is harmless and she will respect the boundaries of me and you."

"Okay I just needed to know."

"I do have a question for you Neema. When I told you to get out of my house, why did you say "Ephesians 5:18?" Dennis asked.

"I have no clue. It just came out of my mouth. That was on my mind and I guess on my spirit as well. You see, the spot where I hit that lady when I was drunk, someone had put up a sign there and that Bible verse was on the sign. Ever since then it has stuck in my mind."

"Wow, I looked it up and I see how it could speak into your life."

"Yes, I needed that wakeup call that God was giving me. If it wasn't for that seed that was planted there is no telling where I would be right now.

"That is so true but I am glad that God is helping you get control of your situation because I like you a lot. I want us to begin to get to know each other better. We will take it slow but I want to see what a relationship will be like with you.

"Me too. I definitely want that." Neema says as she grabs Dennis's hand.

"Do you mean it daddy?" Torii asks as she finally speaks after sitting next to them quietly during their conversation.

"Yes I do but we are going to take it slow. I want to get to know Neema as much as you know her and that will take time."

"Yes!" Torii says as she hugs both of them.

"I feel the same way, Torii." Neema says as she relishes the idea of starting a relationship with Dennis.

"Torii don't you have something that you need to tell Neema?" Dennis asks Torii as she shakes her head yes.

"Neema, I want to tell you that I am sorry for drinking your alcohol. You told me not to and I did it anyway. I am also sorry for causing you and my dad to fight." Torii says and Neema knew it wasn't needed at all because if Neema wasn't careless then none of this would have happened.

"I accept your apology, now let me apologize to you. I shouldn't have left you alone with alcohol. Alcohol is not good for you and I hope you never have a taste for it. I will no longer drink any because it has caused me a lot of pain. I have done some things that I am not proud of because of it. So, do me a favor, if you ever see me drinking again, tell your father and I give you permission to fuss at me." Neema says as she gives Torii a hug.

"Okay I sure will." Torii says as she smiles the smile that Neema has missed over the past month. Neema knew the cause of her pain was the alcohol but now she knows the joy in her life was because of God and how she is relearning to put him first.

*   *   *

"I want to say this again, I do appreciate you and Torii coming with me this morning. It means a lot to me." Neema says as she looks at Dennis who was sitting in the passenger seat. Torii was on her phone barely paying attention to what was being said.

"No problem. You asked us to join you and I feel this could benefit all of us." Dennis says as he looks over at Neema.

Neema knows that she has been tying up loose ends the past few weeks in her life. Once she and Dennis decided to start a relationship, Neema felt like it was the perfect time to renew her relationship with God. Pieces have been falling into place in her life and now she gets what she has been missing out on over the past few years of her drinking. Neema drives and she exits the freeway

because she was on her way to pick up Mrs.
Stanton to take her to rehab. She drives down the
service road until she comes to what she wanted to
show them. Neema stops the car at the
entranceway to Mrs. Stanton's housing area.

"Okay get out, I want to show you
something." Neema says as she turns the car off
and gets out.

"What's up?" Dennis asked.

"Oh man, what happened to that wall?"
Torii says as she points to the wall that Neema hit
with her car and it still wasn't repaired.

"I happened to that wall. That was the
damaged I did to the wall that day I was driving
drunk." Neema says as she shakes her head at
what she did.

"Wow, Neema you could have died." Dennis
says as he looks at the damage to the wall.

"Were you scared?" Torii asks as she grabs
Neema's hand and Neema needed it.

"Yes I was scared but not as scared as the
woman I hit." Neema says as she begins to cry. Her
life could be one thousand times worse if she
would have killed Mrs. Stanton. She could be

serving a life sentence for that but God spared her and Mrs. Stanton.

"This is where you got the verse from?" Dennis asked as he looked up at the sign.

"Yes. Someone obviously felt the need to let the world know and I am glad they did."

"That is powerful to change someone's thinking and life with one verse from the Bible." Dennis says as he looks at Neema.

"I am glad you and that lady didn't die. I would be real sad if you were gone." Torii says as Neema lets her tears fall on her face. Dennis walks over and puts an arm around Neema. As she stands here she is really understanding how blessed she was to walk away with only a few aches and pains. There was a reason she was spared and Neema was understanding that more every day.

"I am glad too but I have to relive this very accident twice a week. You see when the judge handed down the sentence, he knew what he was doing. I am reminded of my mistake everyday as I pass by here to pick up Mrs. Stanton. Yes, I would have remembered it if I had gotten jail time but there is something about literally being at the spot where damage was done that puts things into perspective. To make things worse is not only do I have to relive it but so does Mrs. Stanton. She has to not only see the spot but she feels it every day she wakes up and has to get her body back to normal."

"I know it is tough on you Neema but I want to encourage you to be strong and do whatever it takes to make the situation better." Dennis says as he tries to help Neema cope with what she is feeling.

"I am doing that. I try my best to be as nice and caring for Mrs. Stanton but I am afraid that the damage is done and she might not ever forgive me. I will understand if she doesn't." Neema says as she thinks about the past month and a half of taking Mrs. Stanton to rehab and how they have a lot of bad days and a few good ones. Their interaction is not always pleasant and Neema can't expect it to be. Not after what she did to change Mrs. Stanton's life forever. It would be selfish of her to expect Mrs. Stanton to overlook the obvious to spare Neema's feelings. Neema has to remind herself that she isn't the victim but Mrs. Stanton is.

"I know you feel helpless when it comes to the feelings that Mrs. Stanton has towards you. Just keep doing the Christian thing by showing love and God will be pleased with you." Dennis says as he squeezes Neema.

"I just want her to know that I am truly sorry. I tell her but she doesn't believe me and it hurts because I know I did something terrible and I would never deny it. I just want her to treat me nice for once." Neema says as she realizes she has never told anyone what was bothering her. In her mind, this was her prison sentence and no one wants to be in prison with her so she just dealt with it. She feels better getting it off of her chest.

"It's going to be okay. Let's just pray on it and leave it in God's hands." Dennis says as he begins to pray for Neema. She needed it more than ever. She knows that she is truly remorseful and feels bad for the damage she has caused.

"Thank you Dennis for praying. I have been praying for her as well because she is the one that is really suffering. I am only having a pity party but she is the one that is living it."

"Well we need to shut your pity party down. We need to not worry about things that are out of our control. You are doing all you can so focus on what you can control and that is how you react to how Mrs. Stanton acts."

"You are right Dennis. Come on guys we need to go and get Mrs. Stanton. I don't want to be late." Neema says as they walk back to her car. Dennis and Torii get in the back.

"She is just right here around the corner." Neema says as she turns the car on and begins to drive into the entranceway. Neema has gotten use to how the area looks. Only a few months ago she looked down on what she sees now. After coming here on a weekly basis and seeing, parents walking their children from the bus stop. Husbands and wives going to and from work as some come home in uniforms. Men and woman jump roping and playing games with children in the street has shown Neema that her misconceptions about the area was her perception from what she saw on the news. Yes there are still bad folks that live in this area but for the most part it is just people trying to make a living doing it one day at a time. Neema feels embarrassed that she thought so little of people she knew nothing about. Neema sees Mrs. Stanton house as soon as she turns on her street. Today was different because Mrs. Stanton was already sitting on the second step of her porch as Neema drove past her house so she could turn the car around so the passenger side was closes to the sidewalk. Neema stops and puts the car in park. Mrs. Stanton just sat there looking at the car.

"Want me to go help her?" Dennis asked.

"Nope. She doesn't like to be helped. The only person she has allowed to help her is the rehab nurse, since she doesn't use the walker that often." Neema says as she just watches to see what Mrs. Stanton does next.

"Well I will go help her then." Torii says as she jumps out the car.

"Wait Torii." Neema says but Torii ignored her and walked right up to Mrs. Stanton with no fear at all. As soon as Torii reached Mrs. Stanton, a large smile appeared on her face. She began to engage Torii in a conversation. They were talking like long lost friends when Mrs. Stanton looks over at the car and pointed. She looks back at Torii and they began talking again.

"What in the world could they be talking about?" Neema asks as she tries to read Mrs. Stanton's lips.

"With Torii, there really is no telling." Dennis replies.

After a few minutes of them talking, Torii grabs Mrs. Stanton by the arm and helps her down the sidewalk to the passenger side door. Torii opens the door and Mrs. Stanton begins her normal routine to get into the car. She sits down and closes the door. Torii walks to the other side of the car and gets in.

"Mrs. Stanton, this is Dennis and you have already met Torii." Neema says as she points to Dennis.

"Hi. That is a delightful young lady you have there. She is so smart and pretty. We wouldn't want her to do anything dumb when she gets older like some people we know." Mrs. Stanton says as Neema's jaw dropped. Neema couldn't believe that Mrs. Stanton would say that in front of Torii and Dennis.

"Hey!" Torii says from the backseat.

"What baby?" Dennis asked.

"Mrs. Stanton knows what I am talking about." Torii says as she shakes her finger at Mrs. Stanton.

"I just had to get one more in." Mrs. Stanton says as she and Torii start to laugh. Neema and Dennis just sat there stunned because they didn't know what was going on.

"What are you talking about?" Neema asks as she begins to drive.

"I have spoken to Torii and she told me a few things I have found to be rather interesting. She told me how you are a role model for her and that you made a mistake that you are truly sorry for. She also said that you are doing everything you can to make up for what drinking has cost you and then she asked me something.”

"What was that?” Neema asked because she was curious as to what Torii asked Mrs. Stanton that would cause her to talk to Neema. Normally she would just look out the window as they drove to the rehab center.

"She asked me to forgive you.” Mrs. Stanton says as the car goes silent. Neema didn't know what to say and she can tell that caught Dennis totally off guard.

"And what did you say?” Torii asked even though she already knew the answer.

"I said that I had already forgiven you a long time ago.” Mrs. Stanton says and Neema felt her heart leap. She had been wondering how Mrs. Stanton truly felt about her but she was too scared to say anything.

"So why have you been so harsh with me?” Neema asked with courage that has caught her off guard.

"Well, I have forgiven you but I was still angry and bitter. I was so mad that it took over my spirit and I became what I felt and that is so unlike me.

"I am sorry for what I have done to you Mrs. Stanton. I have told you that time and time again." Neema adds.

"I know but anyone can say they are sorry but not everyone takes the extra effort to change their ways when what they have done has affected someone else. I was waiting on tangible things you needed to do to show that you were sorry. When you went to AA and began to seek help, I knew you were on the right path. I wanted to see if you were going to stick with it and you have so far and for that I am proud of you."

"Thank you Mrs. Stanton because that means a lot to me." Neema says as she enjoys their first positive conversation since she started taking her to rehab.

"That's not all. Torii also told me that you are going to church now. That means that you get it and that you are trying to better yourself. I like that you are changing by getting more mature and getting a good foundation by having God in your life." Mrs. Stanton says as she finally uses the sweet voice she gives everyone else and not the harsh tone that she normally uses on Neema.

"You can thank Dennis for that. He ensures that I am on the straight and narrow and that I do all I can to get my relationship with God in order." Neema says as she smiles at Dennis.

"Yes, Neema has changed a lot and I hate that it had to be because of all of this before she changed. I can tell you this much, she is truly remorseful for what she has done to you." Dennis says as Neema is so thankful that he was in her corner.

"Neema has been crying over this and everything." Torii adds.

"I knew she was remorseful. Ever since that first day she picked me up, she showed it. She was so nice and polite to me no matter how ugly I was towards her. I kept on pushing her buttons and she kept on taking it. I knew she was trying to deal with me but I was so angry that I didn't care how she felt. I was going to make her feel pain because I felt pain. I have been independent my whole life but I have been stubborn too. One thing I hate more than anything else is change. I had gotten so accustomed to doing everything for myself, that after the accident, I could no longer do those things. So, I naturally attacked Neema because she caused all of this. I was so bitter that I know I wished harm on you and I am just being honest." Mrs. Stanton says as she pats Neema's arm in a tender way.

"I lashed out at you Neema because I felt you took my freedom and my independence from me. That was all I truly had in my life. All my family is in Washington State. I have no children and I have been living here in Houston for twenty five years but I have been alone since my husband passed away over fifteen years ago. It is just me and when I wasn't able to do what I once freely did I felt helpless. It takes me a lot longer to do the things that I know I can do in a heartbeat. I hate that I have to struggle to do everything. I was bitter because I felt helpless and I hate that feeling more than anything else. I have no one to depend on except me. There is no one living with me to help me if I need help. No one to eat meals with or to help clean up. People in the neighborhood stop by for conversation from time to time but it is nothing meaningful. So I am all I have and if I can't do for myself then I am in trouble." Mrs. Stanton says as she looks forward but Neema could hear the emotions in her voice.

"I am sorry for taking all of that away from you Mrs. Stanton. I never meant for any of this to happen. I know I made a terrible mistake and I hope that one day you will be able to be like you once was."

"I know you didn't mean it. I know you didn't wake up on that day and told yourself that you were going to go out and almost kill someone. It's just that I am alone, scared and broke down." Mrs. Stanton says as she holds back the tears in her eyes.

"You won't be alone no more because you have us." Torii says as Mrs. Stanton breaks down crying.

"What did I say?" Torii asked.

"Pull over Neema." Dennis says as he begins to rub on Mrs. Stanton's shoulders. Neema pulls over into a Panda express parking lot.

"Mrs. Stanton I am sorry if I hurt your feelings." Torii says because she didn't know if something she said was bad.

"You didn't do anything wrong Torii. I was crying because I needed to. I had a lot of bad feelings that I kept stored up on the inside and it was time for me to let them go. You see Torii, I am an old woman with no children of my own so I will never be able to have grandchildren. Just talking to you this morning and hearing how sweet and caring you are just makes me wish I had a grandchild of my own."

"That makes me sad."

"Don't be sad Torii. I will be okay as long as you come and visit me sometime." Mrs. Stanton says as she looks back at Torii. Torii looks at Dennis who nodded his head in approval.

"If it is okay with you Mrs. Stanton, we will all come visit you sometimes." Neema says as she is glad that they are on better terms. Neema pulls back on the street since the rehab center was right around the corner.

"That would be sweet if you all visited me. It would be nice to have someone to sit down and talk to." Mrs. Stanton says as she wipes her eyes.

"You see daddy. We are one big family now all I need is some brothers and sisters." Torii says as Dennis started to cough and Neema started to giggle.

"Slow your roll baby." Dennis says as he joins Neema in laughing at Torii's comment. Neema never thought about having children so she quickly dismissed that thought.

Neema pulls into the rehab center parking lot and drives up to the entrance.

"You can park, I have my little friend here to help me walk in." Mrs. Stanton says as she smiles at Neema. Neema obliges her request and she finds a spot in the parking lot.

"I do want to say that I am glad you all came with us this morning. You have just made my day a whole lot better than I thought it was going to be." Mrs. Stanton says as she looks back at Torii and Dennis.

"No problem. As a matter of fact it was Neema's idea to bring us. She wanted us to see what had burden her so much which was the spot of the accident." Dennis says as he takes off his seat belt.

"I can release a burden too by having that sign taken down. I believe it has served its purpose by now." Mrs. Stanton says as she nods her head up and down.

"You were the one to put that sign up?" Neema asked.

"Yes. I had received a flyer in the mail and I called them up. They actually done it for free due to my circumstance."

"No way. That is my job that makes those signs. To make things seem more ironic, those signs were my idea. I thought of that concept and who would ever think that it would be used to get through to me." Neema says as she ponders how God gave her the idea to make the signs knowing that one day the same signs would change her life.

"God knew what he was doing. He let your own works be used against you to prove a point." Dennis says to bring the point home.

"What made you choose that particular verse?" Neema asked.

"I was sitting at home and I was about to do my nightly reading of the Bible. I opened the Bible just randomly and my finger landed on that verse. I read it a couple of times and I got goose bumps because it was so perfect for what I wanted to say and the rest is history."

"God is always working things out for the good. I am glad that one sign ended up blessing you both." Dennis says as he puts his hand on Neema's shoulder.

"We are blessed. I know I am because he has turned my life around and I am so thankful for that. I am glad that God was on my side even when I didn't think I needed him." Neema says as she thinks about how God set up her situation to change her because without his intervention, she would have never changed on her own.

"I want to pray for us." Mrs. Stanton says as she holds out her hand to Neema and Dennis. Torii grabbed their other hand and Mrs. Stanton prayed for them all. It was a long prayer but it was needed.

"We better get in there because we are late." Neema says as she looks at the time.

"Don't worry I will just blame you as always." Mrs. Stanton says as her and Neema shared their first laugh together.

*   *   *

"Okay, I want cheese pizza, French fries and a chocolate shake." Torii says as she looks over the menu.

"Are you going to eat all of that?" Mrs. Stanton asks as she looks over her menu.

"I am because my dad says I am a bottomless pit."

"She is Mrs. Stanton, believe me." Dennis says as he laughs at the thought of how much Torii eats.

"I think I am going to have chicken fried steak, mashed potatoes with gravy, and some corn. I think that will definitely hit the spot." Mrs. Stanton says as she puts her menu down.

"What about you Neema?" Dennis asked.

"I was thinking the turkey sandwich and fries."

"Boring." Torii says as she starts to laugh.

"I know." Mrs. Stanton adds.

"Hey no fair, it is two against one. I know you are on my side, right Dennis?" Neema asked Dennis as he tries to hide his face with his menu.

"I am staying out of this because I was thinking about ordering the same thing."

"No dad you are not supposed to be on Neema's side. I am your daughter so that means you are on my team." Torii says as she hits Dennis on the arm.

"I am on your team. I will always be on your team." Dennis says as he holds Torii's hand.

"No you are not." Torii says as she playfully pulls her hand away from Dennis.

"Neema can I talk to you for a second?" Mrs. Stanton asks as she motions for Neema to get up and follow her.

"Sure." Neema says as she isn't quite sure why Mrs. Stanton wanted to talk to her in private.

Neema follows Mrs. Stanton out the front door to a bench that was out front of the restaurant. Neema looked back in the restaurant to see Dennis and Torii talking and she figured he was trying to explain to her that he was still on her team.

"Yes ma'am." Neema says to let Mrs. Stanton know she was ready to hear what she had to say.

"Neema I wanted to take this time to you let you know you have a wonderful thing going on here. I watched the three of you interact and I know that what I see is genuine. It's special and I am not saying this because I think you would mess it up but I am telling you this because I want you to know that you are blessed. I want you to always think about what you would have missed out on if you had kept on drinking. If God hadn't sat you down and woke you up, you would probably be in jail or dead. He has given you a blessing when you didn't deserve to be blessed. So if there is ever a time you want to drink again, I want you to think of the moment when you felt like you loss them for good and let that motivate you to put that drink down. I have faith that you will be strong enough to not go down that road again but I am not naïve enough to know you won't have days when you will struggle. Continue to lean on God and allow him to give you the strength to fight your battles and not give in." Mrs. Stanton says as she gives Neema a big hug and Neema knew this was the moment she needed more than anything else. Her tears was flowing down her face as she finally realizes what forgiveness feels like in Mrs. Stanton's hug.

"Mrs. Stanton, thank you so much for forgiving me. I know I caused you a lot of pain. I am saying it now but when your rehab assignment is over I still want to keep in contact with you. We can keep the two day a week setup if you like?" Neema asks and she hopes Mrs. Stanton agrees.

"Yes I would like that as long as you bring Torii with you."

"Deal." Neema agrees.

"Let's go eat because all of that rehab has made me hungry." Mrs. Stanton says as she moves faster than Neema has ever seen her before.

"Now you wanna walk fast." Neema says as they start laughing. They walk back into the restaurant and Neema can feel a difference in the air. There is no more tension and Neema welcomed that. She makes it to the table and Torii is smiling.

"I have something to tell you." Torii says as she points at Neema.

"You better not complain about the job the waitress is doing. She just started the job because she is new." Dennis says to get Torii to not speak about it.

"Oh I am so glad you mentioned new job. I have news to tell everyone." Neema says as she can't believe that it slipped her mind.

"Okay but hurry up." Torii says as she gets impatient.

"I will be quick Torii. Okay everyone I was offered a new position at my job and I accepted it." Neema says as she hopes it is good news for them as it is for her.

"Congrats Neema. That is wonderful news." Dennis says as he claps and Torii joins him.

"That is fantastic. Praise God." Mrs. Stanton says as she claps also.

"I do need to inform you guys that the job calls for me to do some traveling and that means sometimes days or a week at a time."

"Oh I see, but we understand. You have worked so hard to move up in the company so don't let nothing stop you now." Dennis says to give her his approval.

"I have to consider two things. One, I won't be able to make all of your rehab appointments and I definitely don't want to go to jail.

"Neema who is going to know. I won't tell them." Mrs. Stanton says as she understands what could happen if Neema missed an appointment.

"How will you get there then?" Neema asked.

"If it is alright with you Mrs. Stanton, Torii and I would take you in the case of Neema not being in town." Dennis says to help Neema out.

"That would be wonderful." Mrs. Stanton says as Torii gives her a high five.

"I sure do appreciate that Dennis and thank you Mrs. Stanton for understanding." Neema says feeling the love.

"I hope you are finished so I can tell you what I wanted to say." Torii says as her patience has run thin.

"It better be good Torii since you are interrupting Neema." Dennis says as he playfully scolds Torii.

"I am sure it is." Mrs. Stanton says as she smiles at Torii.

"Please tell us what is so important."
Neema says as she tries to think what could be so
important.

"Okay, my daddy is on my team."

Omega

WHAT IF?

"Wake up my son."

Lester hears someone talking to him but he can't distinguish if he is dreaming or awake.

"Wake up my son."

Lester hears it again and he doesn't recognize the voice. It can't be his father because he doesn't live with his father. He lives in another city away from his parents. He doesn't have a roommate nor did one of his friends come home with him from the club last night. He drove himself all the way home, which was a mistake because he was so faded by the drinking and partying that took place that he almost didn't make it. Lester tries to focus on the voice but he can't do that due to the bright light that he sees. He then realizes that he is awake and that his eyes are shut. Yet he still sees the bright, piercing light. All of a sudden the light goes away. Lester slowly opens his eyes and raises up until he is sitting up. He was curious to know whom the voice was that told him to wake up. No sooner than the fact he realized he was awake, the voice went away. Now there was only silence. Lester gives his eyes a few seconds to adjust to the dim light that was seeping between the slivers in his blinds. He notices that it wasn't that bright out so it was still rather early in the morning to where the sun hasn't fully broken the horizon. He glances at his watch and he notices that it is only 6:00 am. He had only been asleep an hour and a half. He can recall stumbling through the door at 4:30 am. He also notices the hand stamp he had received from the topless club he was at last night. The letters were big, black letters with a touch of fluorescent yellow and they showed up real well on his light brown skin. "XXX." Lester smiles as he begins to remember a moment that took place at the club. He also notices that he still had on his clothing from last night. He reeked of beer, vomit, and cigar smoke and he didn't know if that was from the beer he wasted on himself, the cigars that was smoked by others around him or if that was the alcohol seeping out his skin and the vomit smell from his mouth.

"Another slamming night out for you Lester." He says as he grabs his throbbing head and plops backwards on the bed. He quickly jumps up because he realized he saw a shape of a man sitting in a chair next to the window. Lester felt that he wasn't drunk just a little hung over so he knew he wasn't seeing things.

"Who are you and what are you doing in my house? Lester says as he stands up. He quickly jumps over the bed and runs to the wall so he could turn on his bedroom lights. He hits the switch and he immediately looks at the place he saw the shape and lo and behold there was a man sitting there. Lester could feel his heart beating fast as he looks at the man. A thought quickly went through his mind. The thought was how long had this person been sitting there? What were his intentions and who exactly was he?

"You have exactly zero seconds to tell me who you are and what in the world you are doing in my apartment." Lester says as he quickly sizes the man up. He notices that he was a rather small-framed man. He looked to be about one hundred sixty pounds and about 5' 9". Lester definitely didn't fear the man because he was 6'1" and an even two hundred twenty eight pounds. He did notice a large scar on the man's forehead. His hair was almost to his shoulders. The hair was thick, curly and black. His skin was a golden bronze complexion. He had black eyes and a medium sized nose. He was handsome and easy on the eyes. He had on what looked like a long sheet that had the neck cut out so his head could be put through it. A rope was being used for a belt. The outfit covered his whole body and Lester could barely make out sandals that were worn by the man. Lester was now no longer scared, he was angry. He felt that this man posed no threat to him so he was going to get answers from him, and call the cops so he can get rid of him. Lester quickly looks down the hallway to his front door. He can visibly see that the door was still locked. He quickly looks next to the man at the window and he sees that it is still intact. Now he was real curious as to how he got in and what he wanted.

"Tell me what you are doing in here."

"My son, don't be so quick to anger."

"Stop calling me son. I am not your son."

"I am beginning to believe that as well."

"Good, so that now we are on the same page. I am going to call the cops and you are going to jail for trespassing." Lester says as he turns and walks towards his dresser that his phone sat on. As he is walking towards the phone he glances at the clock that is next to the phone and it says, "6:00 am". Lester quickly looks at his watch and his watch still said 6:00 am.

"What? That is weird."

"Why is that weird? Is it because time stands still for no man. It does stand still for God."

"What are you talking about?" Lester asks as he feels the man is talking crazy.

"It is as you heard."

"What? That time stands still for no man. I know that because man doesn't control time. I realize that much but what do you mean about it stands still for God? Are you trying to say that you are God? If you expect me to believe that then you are crazy."

"What is so crazy about that?"

"I have seen your kind before. You do something that others can't do. You get people to follow you and then you trick them into joining you and eventually killing themselves. A man was just captured that was dressed similar to you when he went inside someone's house and took the people's daughter. They found him some time later and he was claiming to be some sort of prophet on a mission for God."

"I never said I was a prophet."

"I know you didn't but still you are trying to speak as if you are God or something. You want me to believe that since you are sitting here, time has stopped because you are God. You are here on earth on some spiritual mission and you just so happened to be in my room. Yeah right. You are whacked out. Whatever drugs you are on, you need to share it if it's that good to make you feel this way. I just so happen to know a little bit about the Bible and I know Jesus will come back for all. It doesn't say anything about Jesus was paying house calls to anyone. So that rules out the fact that you are Jesus. So that only leaves psycho."

"You are mistaken because I am Jesus."

"Yeah right. I know it is early but it isn't that early. I got blitzed last night but I am not drunk right now. If you had seen me about five hours ago I might would have believed you but now, oh no. As a matter of fact, just for the sake of arguing. If you are Jesus, let me see the nail marks in your hands and the ones in your feet." Lester says as he walks towards the man. The man raises up his outfit to reveal holes in his feet and as he grips his outfit, Lester can see the cloth through the holes in his hands.

"No way. You can't be Jesus." Lester says as he begins to feel nausea sweep over him.

"My son, it is I." Jesus says as he drops his outfit back over his feet.

"Is this the Rapture? Are you coming back for the saved? They said that you would come back like a thief in the night." Lester rambles as Jesus holds up his hand to silence him.

"This is not the Rapture. I am here because of you."

"Me?"

"Yes, you. Do you not remember calling on me?"

Lester quickly thinks back to last night. He remembers a few things from the topless club and some of the drive home. He knows that he stumbled through the front door and ran to the bathroom because he felt sick. Then it hit him because he remembers calling for God as he was throwing up.

"I don't get it. Everyone calls out to you when they are sick from drinking too much."

"Not everyone is in ministry."

That hit Lester hard. He knew exactly what Jesus was talking about. Lester was the coordinator of the Nursing Home Ministry at his church. He has been doing it for the past three years. Lester realizes that he had also been living a double life. Yes, he has been doing ministry but he hasn't changed his ways at all. He still partied and did exactly what he was doing before he became saved. Lester got saved one day at church and he never told anyone. He didn't tell his co-workers, his family and most definitely not his friends. He didn't want anyone to know he was saved. He didn't feel comfortable telling anyone.

"Are you here to punish me?" Lester asks as he sits down.

"That is not the purpose of my visit."

"What is it then?"

"I am here to spend the day with you."

"Why?"

"You are a representation of my kingdom. You have confessed with your mouth that I am the Son of God. I died on the cross for the sins of man. I was buried and rose again on the third day. You believed that right?"

"Yes."

"Since you are mine and like all good shepherds, I have the need to tend to my flocks. Therefore I am here to do just that."

"Just me?" Lester asked.

"Yes my son."

Lester was scared because that must mean he has done something wrong. If Jesus was making a special visit to him then that meant he wasn't doing what he was supposed to be doing. He also knew that if Jesus was here to spend time with him then he better be on his best behavior. He quickly remembers that Jesus had stopped time.

"You are going to restart time…"

Before Lester could finish saying his statement, Jesus holds up his hand and says, "Time." Lester looks at his watch and it the hands on his watch were moving again. He glances at his clock and it said 6:01am.

"Today, is Friday so I still have to go to work and everything."

"I realize that and I will be there with you also."

"All day?"

"Every moment."

Lester felt real sick now. He knew that he had his whole day planned. It was Friday so he had planned on doing a lot and he also knew that some of the things he planned are not things he should be doing. He felt like he needed to do something in order to get out of going to work. He decided that he was going to pretend to be sick so he wouldn't have to go to work or go through with his plans. All he has to do is call his friends and tell them he was sick and then he would be cleared.

"Jesus, I am not feeling well today." Lester says as he tries to sound sick.

Jesus shook his head and said,

"Lester, I am dismayed by your attempt to fool me."

Lester is immediately reminded of his foolish attempt to fool Jesus. He has lied so much in his life that even lying to Jesus felt right. He knew he was in for a long day.

"Jesus, there is something I need to tell you." Lester says as he feels the need to confess.

"I know already, my child. Let's get your day started."

Lester knew he meant he knew exactly what he was going to say. Jesus knew the plans he had made for the day so there was no need for Lester to inform him of that.

"I am going to take a shower, I will be right back." Lester says as he stands up and walks towards his dresser. He pulls open his top drawer to his dresser. This drawer was the one that he kept his underwear and socks in. As soon as he pulled the drawer open, sitting right on top were a pack of condoms. He also kept them in there also. Lester was having sex with women even though he wasn't married. It never crossed his mind once to even wait until he was married. He felt he should have it as much as he could. That part of his life he wasn't willing to change and now it was in the open. Lester quickly peeks out of the corner of his eye to see if Jesus had noticed them. He couldn't really tell so he quickly tries to stuff them under some of his things that are in there. The more he tried to hide them the more they kept popping back up. He was frantically trying to hide them until they popped up and fell on the ground by his foot. He looked down at them and he realized that they are in plain view of Jesus. Lester looks up at Jesus and he begins to ramble.

"They are for umm, a umm, a friend of mine that sometimes stays over."

Jesus just shook his head up and down. Lester is taken back by it because it seemed that Jesus believed what he had said. He always felt he was a good liar but never that good. So Lester picks up the condoms and he throws them in the wastebasket next to the dresser. He grabs him some underwear and he turns to walk to the bathroom. He walks past Jesus and he was waiting on him to say something. When Jesus didn't say anything Lester was getting a little more confidence.

"I will be right back." Lester says as he walks out of his bedroom and towards his bathroom. He makes it to his bathroom and he turns around to see if Jesus had followed him. He didn't see him so he flicks on the bathroom light and walks in. He closes the door and looks around the bathroom to make sure he was alone. He lets out a deep breath.

"Today is going to be tough." Lester says as he puts his things down and walks to the shower. He turns it on and gets undressed. He steps in and lets the hot water run over his body. He was glad to be taking a shower. He was tired of the way he smelled. He begins to wonder how he was going to go about his day with Jesus by his side. He knows that he says and does a lot of things he shouldn't. How was he going to be able to do those things as well as please Jesus? Lester hopes he can continue to do what he did with the condoms and that's to be quick on his feet with his reasoning. Hopefully it could buy him some needed time. So he quickly showers up and does his daily morning routine. He comes out of the bathroom and heads back towards his bedroom. He walks in and he looks to the spot where Jesus was and he was still sitting there.

"Sorry it took so long."

Jesus just shook his head.

"Let me hurry up and get dressed so I can start my morning off."

"Is this your normal routine?" Jesus asks as Lester walks towards his closet.

"Yes it is. Every morning." Lester replies.

"What about spending time with the Father of all creation?"

 Lester just stood there. He knew what Jesus was talking about. He was referring to him praying to God. It just never dawned on him to do it every morning. He was into the habit of doing it before meals and before he went to bed but that was about the extent of it.

"Yeah. It just slipped my mind, that's all."

Jesus just shook his head.

"I guess we can do it now. Do you want to pray or do you want me to?" Lester asked because he was afraid to pray in front of Jesus.

"It is for your benefit that you lead the prayer." Jesus replies.

"Ok, umm. Let's see." Lester knew praying was not his strong suit. He felt he did it terribly and that was part of the reason why he doesn't do it that often.

"I am not good at this so can you help me?"

"What do you need help with?" Jesus asked.

"I need help with the right wording and everything."

"Your honesty is good but my son you must realize that it is not what you say or how you say it. It is your intent that counts. You can be eloquent and say all the right things but not truly mean it. Pray what's on your heart."

"Ok. God, thank you for umm, this morning. Thank you for Jesus being here today. I hope all goes well. I pray my day is easy. I pray, umm for all the people in the world suffering. I pray for the, umm other Christians of the world. Amen." Lester says as he waits to hear something from Jesus. Jesus just stood there.

"Was that okay?" Lester asked.

"If that was from the heart then, yes."

Lester turns around and he walks into his closet to get himself something to wear. He gets his clothes and he puts them on. He then grabs his keys and wallet off of the dresser.

"Jesus, I am ready if you are."

"My son I am going to let you know that I will be with you but only you can see me. No one else will be able to. Rest assured, I will be right by your side."

"Ok." Lester says as his mood just shot for the worst. He had hoped that other folks would see Jesus and know that is why he is not doing the normal things he does. Since he just found out that they wouldn't be able to see Jesus that throws a monkey wrench in his machine.

"Why is that Jesus? Why won't everyone else be able to see you?"

"My son not everyone knows me."

"A lot of my friends and co-workers know you. They are always saying God this and Jesus that."

"Some of them use my name in vain and not everyone who calls on the Father will enter the gates of Heaven."

Lester begins to evaluate himself and he feels that he is not all that worthy to be able to stand before Jesus now.

"Jesus some of the people that you talk about are better than me. They are more worthy."

"My son, good deeds and a watchful tongue doesn't necessarily aid you in your quest for salvation."

Lester had heard that before so he knew not to question that. Lester walks out of his bedroom and heads down the hallway towards the kitchen. He turns around and he sees Jesus following him. He walks into the kitchen and he stops in his tracks. On top of his kitchen cabinet sat five different bottles of liquor. Lester knew there was no way of hiding the bottles because Jesus was right behind him.

"These are just for show." Lester says as he points to the liquor bottles on the way to the refrigerator.

"What is it showing?" Jesus asked.

Lester was stumped. He wasn't ready for any reply from Jesus because he had let the other lies Lester said slide by without so much a word being said.

"Showing, umm, showing that, I don't know." Lester says as he just stops trying to lie.

"Exactly. This is doing no more for your salvation than having good deeds. You are actually setting the wrong example for those who have no faith. If those without faith don't see anything different from you, who have faith, then why would they want to be saved? They wouldn't feel a need to change."

"That is true. Even a little drink every now and then?"

"Moderation and never in excess if you must. But if you have to ask then you already know your answer." Jesus replies.

"Okay. Let me get my lunch and then we are off. Would you like a sandwich to take with us?" Lester asked.

"My son, I no longer hunger. My Father gives me all I need."

Lester nods his head and he grabs his sandwich he made last night before he went to the club. His routine was such that anytime he goes out he would take care of all the morning duties just in case he would be running late. He grabbed a bag of chips and a soda. He put them in a brown paper bag.

"If you are ready then I am." Lester says as he begins to walk out the kitchen and towards the front door. They pass through the living room and then Lester hears a "ding" coming from his laptop. Lester heart drops. He didn't realize that his laptop was on. Lester takes a look at the screen and as plain as day his screen saver was showing. It brought instant shame to him. There was a lady wearing lingerie, lying on a bed. Lester quickly runs to the laptop and taps the mouse so the screen saver would go away. He goes into his properties and he changes the screen saver to a nice scenic background.

"Sorry about that."

Jesus just shook his head. Lester turns off his laptop and he walks to the front door. He opens the door and waits until Jesus walks out then he shuts it and locks it.

"Aw man. It's going to rain and I just got my car detailed yesterday." Lester complains as he turns and looks at Jesus.

"Ask yourself this. What's more important, rain and the blessings it brings or your car?"

"The rain. I didn't mean it like that. You right." Lester says as he realizes that he isn't helping his cause by talking, so he turns and walks to his car. He gets in his car and he waits on Jesus to get in on the driver side. Lester puts on his seat belt and then he starts the car. As soon as the car started, Lester's radio starts to blast the music from the CD he had playing in the CD player last night. Lester tried to be quick on the draw and turn the radio off but he starts to hit the wrong button and it only makes the music get louder. Lester was real nervous because about time he turned the radio down, you could clearly hear the curse words coming from the artist on the CD.

"Sorry about that."

"Life and death is in the tongue and that goes for those that say it and does that hear it and believe it."

"I just like the music and I don't listen to the words." Lester says in his defense.

"Just like the Bible. You love to say you have read it but you don't follow the words."

Lester just stared at Jesus because he knew that Jesus was slowly putting his life in perspective. He was slowly dissecting each aspect of his life to show him the error in his ways. Lester decided that he needed to be more cautious in everything he does for the rest of the day. So Lester puts the car in drive and he begins his quest of driving to work. Since the radio was off, it was real quiet in Lester's car. Lester decides to put on some music more suitable. So at the next light, he stops and he grabs his CD case and he starts to look for a gospel CD. He flips thru all one hundred thirty four CD's in his collection and not one was gospel related. Lester immediately begins to feel bad.

"Why the sad look, my son?"

"Jesus, I have a ton of bad CD's and not one that praises you or God."

"Now that you realize that, what are you going to do about them?"

Lester knew exactly what Jesus was asking him to do. He wanted to see if Lester was willing to do it.

"Are you asking me to throw them away?" Lester asked even though he knew the answer.

"What do you gain spiritually by keeping them?"

"Nothing, it's just that some of these CD's are my favorites. Some of these have sentimental value to me and they cost me a lot of money."

"What is considered valuable?"

"I mean I spent a lot of money to purchase all of these CD's. Instead of throwing them away, why can't I sell them and get my money back?"

"Have you not read the story of the woman with the alabaster box?"

"I think so."

"Well, when she anointed my head with the expensive perfume that was in the box, some people scolded her harshly for wasting the perfume because they felt she should have sold the perfume and give the money she received to the poor."

"What was wrong with that? She would still be doing a good thing."

"You are no different than the ones that scolded her. The value of the perfume meant nothing to her. The value of what she did was priceless. So I say to you now that the value you hold for the CD's should not be more than the value of the act of getting rid of them."

Lester was hit hard with that explanation. He knew exactly what Jesus meant by what he had said. Lester was thinking selfishly instead of thinking about the greater good that he would do if he gets rid of the CD's. Lester puts the CD case behind his seat on the floor and he begins to drive. He is extra careful to follow all traffic laws. He signals unlike he normally does. He tries to not go over the speed limit. He is on guard for anything the he could do wrong. Once they are on the expressway, two drivers immediately cut him off. Lester can feel his anger rising but he controls it as they continue his journey to work. He can see that his exit is about two miles up the road. Lester feels that he can make it that far without him losing his cool. All of a sudden a car crosses two lanes and gets in front of

Lester's car. The car starts to drive slower than the speed limit. Lester looks to his right and he sees the lane the car came from was empty. The lane next to Lester's car was empty but yet the car chose to get right in front of him and that didn't sit right with Lester. Lester clicks on his signal light and tries to get over to his left but a truck speeds up and it blocks his entryway into that lane. So Lester tries to get over to the right but now there was a car on that side. The car seemed to be going the exact same speed that Lester was going because it was slightly behind the passenger side door. Lester was trapped and to make things worse his exit was approaching. Lester tries to speed up to pass the car on his right but by doing so he was real close to the car in front of him so he had to slow down. The truck on his left speeds off and leaves that lane open. Lester thought about going around the car in front of him by getting in the lane to his left but about time he gets over and pass the car up he would have missed his exit. So Lester decides to slow down and let the car on his right go by so he can get over to the right lane and eventually get off the expressway. In the process of slowing down, Lester realized that the car was still in the same position. Lester looks over and he sees the driver is looking forward and is really not paying attention. Lester slows down some more and the car seems to be doing the same thing. So now Lester is clearly frustrated.

"*MOVE SO I CAN GET OVER, FOOL. EITHER SPEED UP OR SOMETHING.*" Lester screams as he immediately looks at Jesus.

"I am sorry Jesus. It's just that he isn't even paying attention at all. He is just driving alongside my car. It seems like he is purposely doing that and I need to get over so I can exit."

As soon as Lester says that the car exits at the same exit that Lester needed to take.

"See. All of that and he could have let me over so I could have gotten off the expressway. Now I have to take the next exit, make a U-turn and go back." Lester says to plead his point. He quickly gets over into the next lane so the same thing won't happen again.

"My son, have you realized that you were not the only one needing to get off at that exit?"

"Yes, I realize that."

"If you do then you would know that the other driver was no more at fault for you missing that exit."

"He wouldn't let me over."

"Maybe it has less to do with he wouldn't and more or less, you couldn't."

"Huh."

"Meaning you cannot fault others because you cannot accomplish what you set out to do. The other driver had a plan and that plan was to exit at that very moment. You chose to get in the middle lane so you have to deal with what happens because of that choice."

"It was just that he made me so mad."

"You shouldn't let it affect you that way. Always be considerate of others even if it means you have to go out of your way in doing so."

 Lester knew that was the right thing to do and he also felt it was hard for him.

"You are right Jesus. It is not going to hurt me to go a little further." Lester says as he exits the expressway. As they are driving towards the stoplight, Lester spots a homeless man waiting at the light. Lester feels that this is his chance to finally do something right in front of Jesus. So he starts to check around his console in between the driver seat and the passenger seat. He looks all around but he could find no change. He pats his pockets and he feels nothing. He even goes so far as to check his wallet but he found no money at all.

So his plan to impress Jesus was out the window so he decided to at least make his attempt known.

"Man, I was going to give that guy some money but I don't have anything to give." Lester says as he looks at Jesus, waiting on a smile. Jesus looks at Lester and then he looked down at Lester's lunch and then back at Lester. Lester knew exactly what Jesus meant by doing that. He was implying that Lester give up his lunch. Lester sat there thinking because he knew that if he didn't have a lunch with him at work, he wouldn't have enough time to go and get something. His job only allowed the employees a 30-minute lunch and two 15-minute breaks. Lester knew he could not be late a second or he would be written up. All of the food places by his job stayed so packed that it wasn't even worth it to try to make it back in time. So he knew that this was all he had to eat for the day. He had no money on him so he couldn't get anything out of the vending machine. This was a true dilemma because Lester knows how he acts when he is hungry. He gets very irritable and he is not a pleasant person to be around. He definitely didn't want to show Jesus that side of him because he remembers reading that Jesus went forty days and nights without food or water. Jesus wasn't showing attitude after forty days and nights so there would definitely be no reason for Lester to miss one meal and be raw with anyone. So Lester stops at the light and there are about four cars in front of him. He watches the homeless guy get up and starts to walk towards the first car in the row. At the rate of speed the homeless guy was walking, Lester knew that there was a good chance that the light would turn green and the homeless guy will probably turn around and go back to his spot where he was sitting. That would mean that Lester would have a greater chance of keeping his lunch. Lester watches the homeless guy leave the first car and goes to the second one. Lester glances up and he sees the light is still red. The homeless guy leaves the second car and makes his way towards the car in front of Lester's car. He stops and he is engaging the driver in a conversation all the while Lester is wishing the light would turn green. To make matters worse, Lester's stomach starts to growl to remind him that he hadn't eaten breakfast. Lester watches the driver in the car in front of him hand the homeless man some money. Lester looks over at Jesus just to see if he had seen that transaction. Lester wanted Jesus to tell him to keep his lunch since the homeless guy was taken care of. Jesus gave Lester a look that basically said, "What are you waiting on." So Lester rolls his window down. The homeless guy starts to walk towards the car and Lester reaches down and grabs his lunch. The homeless man makes it to the window and Lester hands him the lunch. The homeless man opens the brown paper bag, looks at its contents, and closes it back. He then looks at Lester and says,

"God bless you."

Lester just sat there stunned. He felt he did not deserve that seeing that he didn't even want to give it to the man. Guilt was sweeping over Lester and he began to feel bad.

"Thank you young man." The homeless man says as he walks off. Lester watches the man walk off with his lunch until the light changed to green.

"Verily I say unto you, inasmuch as ye have done it unto on of the least of these my brethren, ye have done it unto me." Jesus says as Lester drives past the homeless man. Lester began to feel a little better. It did feel good to give up something for nothing. Lester knew that he hadn't done much right this morning so he hoped that the rest of the day goes my smoother.

"It is just so hard to tell when they are really in need or just trying to get over." Lester says to strike up a conversation.

"Deception is a mighty tool that will always be able to confuse many. I can tell you this much, he really is in need."

"Is he saved?" Lester asked as he drives along the expressway service road.

"Yes he is. He will be with me for sure."

"I don't understand. Why don't you help him get out of his situation?"

"I just did."

"That was only a sandwich, chips and a drink. That won't last for long."

"It won't but the act of giving it will start a chain reaction in him that will cause him to better his situation."

"Wow. I never thought about it like that."

"One seldom does. Sometimes the true effect of a blessing happens when you are not around to witness it."

Lester had to marvel at how true that statement was.

"Well we are almost there." Lester says as he makes his final turn on the road that leads to his job. Lester began to feel nervous because now he would be faced with his biggest test of all and that was his co-workers and friends. The things he do and say at work are so far from the type of person he displays at church that Lester was already feeling ashamed.

Lester turns into his job's parking lot and he drives around until he finds an open spot. He parks, steps out of his car, and he begins his walk towards the front door. His heart was beginning to speed up. He opens the door and he makes a right so he can go down the long hallway that leads to his cubicle. He just wanted to be able to make it to his desk without talking to anyone.

"Hey Boo."

The first thought that went through Lester's mind was, "so much for that" He knew he had to speak to her so he turns to greet her.

"What's up Val?"

"What you are not happy to see me?" she asks.

"Of course I am." Lester replies as he tries to walk faster. He didn't feel comfortable talking to her. He looked behind her and there was Jesus right there.

"Since we are both here a little early do you want to go in the janitor's closet and do what we do best?"

Lester thought to himself that if he had eaten breakfast this morning, he would have surely have thrown it up. He definitely didn't want to be reminded about that. He had been messing with her on and off for about a year and a half. It was strictly a spur of the moment thing. She has a fiancée and she claimed to love him. Lester never really thought twice about what they were doing because he was attracted to her. Since Jesus was here he had to play it off.

"Stop tripping Val. I don't have time. I have some important things to take care of."

"Oh, too important for me. Ok, see if I give you some again." Val says as she stops walking.

Lester was glad because he didn't want to engage in any more conversations with her. He didn't even look back to see if she was following him. He just kept on walking towards his cubicle. Once he finally turned on his aisle he was relieved to see that his buddy, Steven was not in yet. Steven was one of the people that he normally engaged in un-Christian like conversations with on a daily basis. Deep down inside, Lester wanted him to be sick today. Lester walks inside his cubicle and he plops down in his chair. He closes his eyes and he leans back. He turns around to see that Jesus was sitting on the edge of his desk. Lester knew he was about to embark on an adventure that was unlike any others.

"What it is my boy?" Steven says as he walks into Lester's cubicle.

No sick day for Steven today.

"What's up? Lester replies.

"I tell you what's up. You were a king last night. You had all the Dirty Leg's all over you. For the first time in my life, I wanted to be you." Steven says as he pats Lester on the back. Steven was speaking about the dancers at the topless club they were at last night. Dirty Legs was the term they used for the dancers. Lester begins to see some of the flashbacks from last night. He did have a lot of fun but he knew it was not the kind of fun he should have been having. Unlike last night, he is feeling guilty and ashamed. He has to relive last night at the worst of times.

"What do you have to say man?"

Lester really wanted to tell Steven to just leave him alone and come back some other time but that wouldn't do for Steven. He was one of the most persistent guys Lester had ever meant.

"I am not up to it right now. I will talk to you later on."

"What? You would usually rub it in my face. Every time you have a wonderful night all you do is talk about the things you did."

"I don't feel up to it today."

"Are you sick?" Steven asked.

Lester was glad Steven asked him that because now he saw his chance to end this conversation.

"Oh yeah. I had way too much to drink and I didn't really eat breakfast this morning so my stomach is messing with me."

"Ok but you just seem different. You are not having second thoughts about what you did last night?"

Little did Steven know that was exactly what was going on. Lester was definitely regretting last night and he wasn't about to talk about it.

"Of course not. I just don't feel well." Lester said as he glances at Jesus. Jesus just shook his head.

"Alright then I will holla at you later." Steven says as he walks out of Lester's cubicle and heads towards his. Lester was glad to see him leave. Lester was not about to entertain anything that wasn't going to make him look good. So for the next six hours, Lester kept to himself.

* * *

"My man. You sure have been quiet all day. Are you sure everything is okay?" Steven says as he walks in Lester's cubicle.

"I'm cool. I just want to make it through the day so I can go home and get me some rest."

"So you are not going to go to happy hour with us? Steven asked.

"No, I am not going to make it."

'You have got to be kidding me? You haven't missed happy hour in two years." You must really be sick then."

"Pretty much."

"That is too bad especially seeing that Joyce was going to be there."

As soon as Lester heard that name, he immediately became conflicted. Joyce was Steven's cousin and he had been trying to hook them up for months. Tonight was going to be their first official date. They had only been talking on the phone but their conversations were hot and heavy. Lester was very much looking forward to their first date. He had seen pictures of her and he knew that he had some plans to be with her. He wanted so badly to go.

"Let me think about it then." Lester says as he puts his face in his hands. He knew he was thinking about what he should do.

"Okay but you need to let me know so I can call and tell her to come or not. She has called me twice today since you haven't been answering your phone."

"I haven't been able to do much today. I am just trying to get over this sick feeling I have."

"I hope you do because you are acting weird today. I kept glancing over here at you and I see you talking to yourself and carrying on."

Lester knew he was referring to the fact that he had been having conversations with Jesus all day. Since Steven couldn't see Jesus, Lester knew how that could look weird.

"My bad."

"Anyway let me know in an hour." Steven says as he walks out of the cubicle.

Lester looks over at Jesus and he sees him staring at him.

"My son, are you ashamed of me?"

"No."

"If that is so then why you have not told them the reason why you are acting the way you are."

"I am sick."

Jesus gave Lester a look that says, "Who are you fooling."

"I am sorry Jesus. I don't know why I won't tell him the truth." Lester says once he realizes that there is no fooling him.

Lester knew he was afraid to tell Steven because of the way he has been acting. Steven has witnessed him do some sinful things.

"Jesus, Steven has witnessed me do some things that would make me look bad if I told him the truth."

"Anything other than telling him the truth is denying me."

Lester knew that was true and he knew that he shouldn't be ashamed to say that he was saved. Lester has spent the whole day learning things that he needed to do in life. He realizes his shortcomings and it all begins with him putting his faith on the back burner.

"I am going to tell him right now." Lester says as he gets up and he motions for Steven to come over.

"What's up? You changed your mind?" Steven asks as he steps in the cubicle.

"No. I am not going tonight."

"Okay. I am going to call Joyce right now and tell her."

"There is something else I need to tell you."

"What's up?"

"Steven, I know I have done some crazy things since we have been hanging out."

"You know it."

"Well, I want to tell you now that I won't be doing those things anymore."

"What are you talking about, Lester? Why are you tripping?"

"Well, basically I have been acting exactly the way I should not have been. I got saved a few years ago. I never told you or anyone. I just kept on acting the way I had always done. I didn't want anyone to know because I didn't want anyone to throw my shortcomings back in my face."

The second Lester said that he realized exactly what had taken place. That was the answer to the reason why. He didn't know how to handle criticism.

"Man, all you had to do was say something."

"I know but I was just being stupid."

"Yeah man because you shouldn't play with God. That's why I haven't gotten saved because I am not ready. I still have some things I want to do. I will one day but not right now."

"Steven you are not promised tomorrow."

"Lester I am so healthy. I am not even worried about dying. I know it is not my time."

"What makes you so sure? Anything could happen at any time. Don't you watch the news? There is such a thing as being a victim. Think about it. I am not trying to scare you but you need to think about your salvation."

"I have thought about it but I don't know if I am ready to give up everything."

"Don't worry about what you give up but think about what you gain and that is access to Heaven. You can't get there no other way. You can't just do good or be nice."

"What do I need to do then?"

"I will tell you Steven and then we can hold each other accountable as we work on doing things that we need to do."

"That's a plan. As long as you help me because it is going to be hard."

"It's going to be hard for me too. That's why it's best that we let others know so they can help us too." Lester says as he gives Steven some dap.

"Let me go finish up my work and let's meet in the boardroom at 5:00 pm so we can handle up on helping me."

"Bet. I will see you then." Lester says as he watches Steven leave. He takes a deep breath and he realizes that it really wasn't that bad telling Steven.

"My son, I am proud of you. You have taken a step in the right direction. Now it is time for me to leave."

"Why?"

"I have accomplished my task."

"I am going to need your help. I need you here with me." Lester pleads.

"Haven't you realized that I am always with you? I am always by your side and just because you couldn't see me that doesn't mean I wasn't there. So therefore I am leaving because you understand now and that was what I had set out to do. So I am going to leave you some advice, stay in the word and always pray, and most importantly share the Gospel. Bye my son." Jesus says as he fades away. Lester stood there for a second and then he realizes how fortunate he was for what took place.

MY QUESTION IS THIS; IF JESUS CHOSE TO SPEND TIME WITH YOU WHAT WOULD YOU CHANGE? WHAT WOULD YOU DO DIFFERENTLY? WOULD YOU STILL GO TO THE SAME PLACES? WOULD YOU TALK THE SAME? WOULD YOU BE YOU OR WOULD YOU CHOOSE TO BE HOW YOU ARE SUPPOSED TO BE AND THAT IS CHRIST-LIKE?

Other books by Cederick Stewart

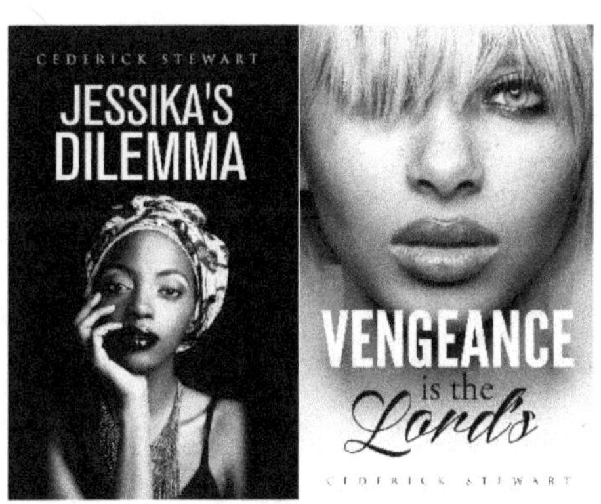

www.ingramcontent.com/pod-product-compliance
Lightning Source LLC
Chambersburg PA
CBHW061249210726
48293CB00003B/907